JUST A CARPENTER

A ROMANTIC ADVENTURE

BILL SILFVAST

PUBLISHED BY SIGMA PRESS • MEDFORD, OREGON

Just a Carpenter
By Bill Silfvast

I dedicate this novel to my wonderful wife Susan, my editor, my companion, and my lover.

～

CHAPTER 1

O n a late spring Friday afternoon in Southern Maine, the construction of a new house was underway.

"David, could you help me lift this heavy roof truss onto the upper framework. You take one end and I'll take the other."

"I've got it, Tom," he said as he grabbed his end and slowly hoisted it above his head.

Suddenly David felt it slipping.

"Watch out," Tom yelled.

"Damn!" David cried as the truss glanced off his shoulder and bounced to the floor. He hunched over, grasping his shoulder in pain.

Tom put his end down and ran over to David, yelling, "Hey man, are you alright?"

"I guess so," David said as he sat on the floor rubbing his shoulder.

He began to stand up while slowly rotating his arm. "It's not too bad."

"You'd better take the rest of the day off ."

"You're right. I won't do much good hanging around here."

Describing the accident to his boss, he said he'd be leaving . It was the middle of the afternoon, so he could drive UBER for the rest of the day.

He removed his tool belt and walked carefully through the rutted construction tracks leading to the street. As he approached his car, he noticed how dirty the other workers' cars and trucks were. He always kept his clean in case he wanted to pick up a few dollars driving Uber on his way home.

As he climbed in, the roses he'd put in the vase attached to the dashboard cheered him up. He tried to keep the vase filled with flowers from his garden when available, enjoying them even when he didn't have passengers.

During the afternoon he managed to pick up a few customers and was near the airport when he received an UBER text. It was a woman named Melanie and the pickup was at the terminal. This would be his last passenger of the day.

Approaching the glass-enclosed airport structure, he admired the large portico, designed to shelter people from the rain and the blinding Maine blizzards.

There were people loading or unloading luggage and frantically scurrying around looking for rides. He was glad he wasn't one of them.

His passenger would have the description of his car and license plate so the pickup should go quickly. The older model metallic green Honda CRV with the spare tire attached to the rear deck lid would be easy to spot. Customers could expect a reliable ride since he always kept the car in good condition.

He noticed an attractive woman exiting the terminal carrying a large black bag slung over her shoulder. She wore a gray business suit, including a skirt. The cream-colored scarf folded artistically around her neck enhanced her looks. He guessed she was no more than five six and seemed to be struggling with the bag.

As she was heading his way, he noticed her hair tied in a bun, highlighting the high cheekbones of her attractive face. She was obviously looking for her ride. What luck, whoever got to pick her up.

He was surprised when she suddenly leaned over the fender and peered through the windshield, giving him a friendly wave.

He noticed the beautiful deep-set brown eyes and a warm smile.

She approached the rear door and pulled it open. "Hi. I think you're my Uber driver. Everything checks from my end."

"If you're Melanie, you're in the right place. Where can I take you?" How could I be so lucky?

"I'm heading home. The address is 94 Rackleff Street here in Portland. I hope you know where that is?"

"I do. Climb in and I'll get you there as quickly as possible," although he preferred not to be in a hurry.

She threw her shoulder bag onto the seat, slid in, snapped the seatbelt in place, sat back, and sighed. "It's so good to relax. It's been a wild day."

She noticed the car was clean, with attractive gray leather seats and also fresh white roses in a cup attached to the dashboard. A nice touch.

He looked like an interesting guy with a Robert Redford look, ruggedly handsome with a shadow beard. He must spend time outdoors, she presumed. Dark blond hair, parted on the side and partially hanging over his bright blue eyes, gave him a sexy appearance. His calloused hands were worker's hands but his fingernails were clean. And an attractive green plaid flannel shirt and clean jeans gave him a relaxed and casual appearance.

They pulled away from the curb, circling around the terminal past the rental car facilities and airport hotels and on to Westbrook Street, continuing into town.

"Do you drive Uber full-time?"

"No, but it provides extra money and I get to meet interesting people, like you."

"So what do you do most of the time, as a profession I mean?"

"I'm a woodworker. My main interest is designing and making unique furniture, but I can't make enough money at it. Maybe I'm too fussy. So I work as a carpenter, building houses."

"It's important to love what you're doing."

"I agree. So where did you just come from?"

"I was in New York on a consulting job."

"That's quite a change from Maine."

"It is. And that's why I live here. I don't care for the big city life."

"Then what took you to the city?"

"I'm a graphic designer. I design layouts that are part of the advertisements that make you want to buy something."

"I can blame you for the things I have around the house that I know I can't live without, but never use?"

She laughed. "Yes, I'm one of the culprits. But it's a very challenging, competitive business and I guess I'm good at it. At least some people think I am, because they're willing to pay me."

"You get to live where you want and do what you want."

"I do. But I wish I didn't have to go to big cities to make presentations and attend meetings."

Driving on Route 302 he made a left turn to get to Rackleff Street.

"Even though you can't make a living at wood working, it's nice that you find the time to do it. I think everyone should have something that challenges them."

While traveling along Stevens Avenue at thirty miles an hour, an old blue Ford pickup truck ran the stop sign and came speeding towards them.

"Watch out," he yelled as he hit the brakes, swerved to the side of the road, spinning halfway around, the Ford narrowly missing them. He came to an abrupt stop as the truck sped off. The air bags didn't deploy and his head and chest were thrown against the steering wheel.

"Wow! That was close!" he whispered.

Collecting himself, he immediately turned towards his passenger.

She was leaning forward with her hands on the back or the front seat. He reached for her left hand and held it. "Are you okay?"

She squeezed his hand and looked up. "I…I think so. What happened?"

"That guy ran a stop sign."

"That was too close for comfort." They grasped hands for a few moments, occasionally sharing eye contact.

Another driver stopped and knocked on David's window. "Are you both okay? That was a close call."

David lowered his window and hesitatingly said, "Yes, I think we'll be fine. Thanks for asking."

Turning back towards Melanie and grasping both of her hands, he saw a very serious face.

She broke into a weak smile and whispered "Thank you," as she gave his hands another squeeze. "I think you saved our lives."

"It was a close call. Are you ready to continue to Rackleff Street?"

"I think so. But drive slowly. I've never experienced anything like this in my life."

"I don't think I have either."

They pulled up to a two-story white shake house that had a peaked roof and a third story attic window. The covered front porch provided the backdrop for a small well-mowed lawn and attractive shrubs. The walkway to the front porch consisted of large irregular-shaped gray flagstones, surrounded by white gravel.

He quickly slipped out of his seat, hoping to get to her door before she had a chance to open it, possibly getting a glimpse of her legs. He pulled it open and said, "May I help you?"

"Well, sir. I haven't had this kind of service for quite a while."

As she slid out, he wasn't disappointed. He grasped her carry-on bag and followed her along the walkway and up the steps to the porch, where they faced a beautifully carved solid oak front door.

"How are you doing? That was quite an experience."

"I'm settling down. I'll be okay."

He handed her the shoulder bag, temporarily holding her hand. "I'm so sorry this happened. I hope you don't think it was my fault," he said, looking into her eyes.

"Definitely not. You're my hero!"

"I don't know about that, but I pride myself on being an alert driver." Looking around he said, "I love your carved wood front door and the trim color. Are you the one who selected it?"

"I am. And I think the trim fits in very well with the coloring on the neighborhood houses."

He turned and momentarily glanced along the street. "I agree."

She reached into her purse for the key and also pulled out a five-dollar bill.

"Oh, you don't have to do that. The tip is included in the fare."

"I understand it's possible to add a supplement for extra good service. That's what I received today."

"Thank you. It was a close call. I guess I'll be on my way," he said hesitatingly. He turned and headed slowly towards the street. Why did he hate to leave?

She took in his muscular body. Probably around six two, very trim. And a confident but unassuming walk.

When he got into his car he noticed she was still standing in the doorway so he waved as he climbed in.

Melanie waved back and went into her front hall where the walls were covered with nicely hung pictures. Fresh flowers occupied vases on small tables on both sides of the entryway. Zelda's work she surmised.

Such an interesting, soft-spoken man. And that brief moment when they were holding hands was so comforting. It felt like a magnet between them.

Standing there for a moment, she called, "Zelda, I'm home. It's okay for you to leave now."

Zelda poked her head around the kitchen doorway. "Thanks Miss Melanie. I hope you had a good trip. I'll be here for the kids on Monday unless I hear from you."

"Thanks, Zelda. You're so helpful. What would we do without you?"

No sign of her kids so she slipped into the dining room, dropped her bag on one of the oak chairs surrounding the large antique table, and sat down next to it. Normally it would be a very inviting room but it felt empty. Was she really glad to be home?

"I don't even remember his name but I think I have it on my Uber text," she mumbled.

She got out her cell phone and retrieved it: David. Nothing revealing about that. So what intrigued her about him? Not only was he attractive, but he was kind and sensitive and also focused on what he liked to do.

He was different from Paul who only wanted to watch sports, either on TV or at the ball park. Paul was a good husband, she thought, but his life revolved around sports. He spent time with the kids when there wasn't a game on TV. And the two of them occasionally went out for dinner with friends.

He had a good job as an accountant so she certainly didn't have to worry about money or about him spending time with a bad group of guys or another woman. That's not who he was. And her income was almost as much as his so they were able to put away a good amount for retirement. But retirement to do what she wondered?

She kept trying to tell herself she was content, but was she? Heading upstairs, she carried her bag over her shoulder while holding on to the oak banister.

CHAPTER 2

Melanie walked into her bedroom. The light green walls with the colorful flowered soffit patterns usually cheered her up, but not today. She threw her bag on the soft duvet-cover and began unpacking, feeling a bit disconcerted. She tried to settle down, still thinking about the Uber experience. She was focused more on her reaction to him as a person than a driver, although he was very good at driving. He seemed to be a nice man, unassuming and certainly not unattractive.

Enough of that. On with getting her bag unpacked. It didn't take long. After changing into her jeans and a white t-shirt, she reached to remove her pearl earrings. The left one must have just fallen off or maybe it was in the dining room. A look on the floor was unsuccessful.

She looked again while on her way downstairs and also where she'd sat at the dining room table. No luck. She'd make a note to check more closely in the morning.

The antique grandmother clock near the front door indicated it was 5:30, enough time to put a dinner together rather than grabbing something from the freezer.

The ground beef Zelda had purchased helped her with the menu, meat sauce with spaghetti. Also she'd slip a French loaf into the oven, buttered and sprinkled with garlic. Did David like to cook, she wondered? Why was she concerned about that?

Josh came drifting into the kitchen, probably having been

glued to the TV, she thought. And Nellie was most likely in her room texting.

"Hi Mom, what's for dinner?" Josh said. "Um. Looks like spaghetti. I hope we get some garlic bread."

"You certainly do. Have you been behaving yourself while I've been away?"

"You know I always behave, Mom."

"And did Nellie get to her soccer practice yesterday?"

"Yeah, she went with Judy and her mom."

"We'll be eating as soon as Dad gets home so don't run off."

She peeled and chopped the onions and garlic and sautéd them in a hot pan. Next came the chunks of hamburger, a can of chopped tomatoes, and salt and pepper. She let the mixture simmer before putting it in the fridge. It could be reheated along with the spaghetti as soon as Paul told her he was ready to eat.

If David was so creative in designing furniture, he must like to cook. Why was she even thinking about him? It was just an Uber ride, or was it?

Shortly after six, Paul came in through the side door. He approached Melanie, gave her a quick kiss on the cheek and then went over to Nellie, who had just come into the kitchen, wrapping his arm around her and gave her a big hug.

Turning to Melanie, he said, "How was your trip to the big city? Did you sell them on your ideas? I'm sure you did since you always do."

"I did indeed. They loved them and also liked my presentation, so it was a productive trip. But I missed all of you while I was away. I hope Zelda fixed good dinners."

"She did, Mom. One night we had pizza and the other night a chicken pie of some sort that had vegetables in it. It was OK, but the pizza was great."

"She did a good job but we missed your cooking," Paul chimed in.

Only my cooking, she noticed.

"I'll get out of these clothes and be ready for my scotch. Could we be finished by 7:30? The Red Sox are playing at Fenway Park."

"I'm sure we can fit the dinner in before your game."

She wondered what David would be doing. Probably heading for his workshop and the peace it provided.

While the game was on she'd head up to her office in the spare bedroom. It was a comfortable place with a small oak desk and chair, located next to an easel. Also a brown queen-sized sofa-bed for guests, and a reclining brown leather chair that she loved to relax in. She could either read or watch a small TV. It was her game hangout. Men had man caves. She had her game hangout.

Paul came bounding down the stairs and into the kitchen, filled a cocktail glass with ice, and headed for the mahogany bar cart in the dining room. He poured three fingers on the rocks and moved to the family room, not saying anything in the process.

Melanie took a wine glass from the oak hutch and poured a glass of Chardonnay. Wandering into the family room, she sat next to Paul who gave her a quick peck on the cheek. He clicked his glass with hers before turning back to the TV. After the six-o'clock news finished, she returned to the kitchen to get dinner ready.

"Dinner is on," she soon announced, and the family came quickly. Everyone was hungry, especially for her homemade spaghetti and garlic bread. Both she and Paul had a glass of Chianti, and the kids enjoyed their milk.

Promptly at 7:30 Paul was off to the family room for the game. The room was open to the kitchen with pine paneling on one wall, bookcases lining another, and large sliding glass doors opening to the patio.

Melanie loved to curl up on the L-shaped brown leather sofa, especially at times when the TV wasn't blasting, her feet resting on the oak coffee table that was generally covered with magazines.

After dealing with the dishes she sat down at the end of the couch with the kids, learning about what had gone on at school. At 9:00 she encouraged them to go to bed.

Her activity on game nights, which was most nights, was to migrate to her hangout. Settling into her leather lounge chair, she curled up with a good book, a romantic novel. Why did she choose that type of book? Probably the same reason so many women purchase the tabloids at the supermarkets. To add a little spice to their lives.

Melanie thought about her ride home. Just another Uber? Definitely not! Something seemed to connect between her and the driver. The way he looked at her. She'd never had anything like that happen before.

CHAPTER 3

As David sat in his car he realized something had just happened between him and Melanie! The way she looked at him when they were holding hands. She even stood at the doorway and waved as he got in the car. That certainly never happened before with a customer.

He put the car into drive and pulled slowly away from the curb. All kinds of thoughts were going through his head. She was such an intriguing person. And very attractive. But the feeling was more than that. Something they both recognized. And the look he saw in her eyes.

Enough! He headed for home on the outskirts of Portland, a fairly open area with a scattering of oak trees. People had constructed small, inexpensive houses typically on an acre of land. As soon as he and Ginny were able to purchase the land, he started building their house, mostly by himself but hiring out the plumbing and electrical work. It was a natural shake house with a gabled roof.

Evenings and weekends of construction had kept him busy but he'd finished the job five years ago. They'd been living comfortably there ever since.

He drove down the driveway, past his house, and parked in front of the large cedar-shingled garage that served as his wood shop.

He'd saved every penny for several years to purchase his

woodworking tools. All the tools were second hand but that was all he could afford. There wasn't a routine he couldn't do with them.

He admired the small sign on his shop door, The House of David, a catchy phrase that he thought had a religious connotation. Good marketing. He was familiar enough with the scriptures to feel comfortable with it.

With the weekend arriving, he'd be able to get back to furniture making. He was working on a new chair design, the type that could either be used as part of a set, or as an occasional piece.

When he entered the house a warm feeling engulfed him. It was the smell of dinner cooking. Ginny was such a good cook. But it was also the feeling that he had built their home himself.

"Hi honey, how was your day?" He gave her a kiss on the cheek.

"The usual. Driving the kids to their activities and picking them up. I did attend a meeting that dealt with a proposal to decrease the daily limit on the number of lobsters that can be caught. It was *Save the lobsters* versus *Save the jobs*. The usual arguments. How was your day?"

"I got off early from the construction site so I drove Uber for a few hours." He chose not to mention his shoulder since it felt much better.

"My last trip was very scary. A pickup truck ran a stop sign at high speed and almost hit us broadside. I spun out as I swerved to the side of the road and he missed us. My passenger and I were in shock for a few minutes, but we recovered and I got her home safely."

"A woman? Was she good looking?"

"Not bad. She was a business woman returning from a presentation in New York. She develops ads that make people want to buy things; a job I'd certainly not want to have."

"Me neither. Why don't you get yourself cleaned up for dinner?'

"Do I have time for a beer first? I need something to calm me down after that near miss."

"Go ahead. I made a lamb stew."

"Sounds great."

He grabbed a beer from the fridge and headed for the family room where his kids were glued to the TV. His reclining chair was waiting. Thinking about the near accident, he wondered what Melanie was doing? Probably making dinner. I'll bet she's a good cook since she has an artistic flair. She would have to be quite creative to do well in her job.

It wasn't long before Ginny called the family to dinner. While eating, she turned to David. "I have a meeting tonight so it's your turn to be with the kids."

"What meeting is that?"

"It's the recycling committee. Why they're having it on a Friday evening, I don't know."

"OK. I was planning to work in the shop but I'll delay that until tomorrow. I'll be driving Uber in the morning, so I'll head out to the car now and clean it up before you leave."

"That will be in about half an hour."

He was sitting on one of the rear seats, wiping off the leather with a damp rag when he began to ponder his life. He was just a carpenter building houses, but woodworking was where his heart was. His wife and two children were important, but they didn't stir up his feelings the way creating a new wood design did. Was that normal for a 15-year marriage? His wife was pleasant and attractive, but that didn't lead to many romantic interludes. She had her agenda, he had his, and they didn't usually coincide.

He looked forward to evenings and weekends when he could do what he loved, designing and building beautiful furniture. It was the beauty of the wood, the way the grains flowed in various directions, not guided by any prescribed program. Independence leading to beauty.

As he was vacuuming, he noticed something on the floor in front of the right rear seat. Leaning over, he picked up a pearl earring. It must be Melanie's, he decided, since his previous customers were all men.

He'd take it to her in the morning. Why was he excited about that? Was losing her earring just a coincidence?

He put the earring in a small cardboard box. He also put his Uber card, including his personal cell phone number, in the box, and also his furniture business card. A little advertising wouldn't hurt.

Back in the house, he settled into his lounge chair with a pad of paper and pencil and spent the rest of the evening sketching furniture designs while the kids watched TV.

CHAPTER 4

Melanie was up early Saturday morning. A golf day for Paul. She'd put his bagels out the night before and he could make his favorite coffee in the Keurig. She'd planned a Saturday breakfast with the kids. Sometimes Paul was included but golf always came first.

The menu was waffles, fried eggs, bacon, and maple syrup. Also juice, hot cocoa for the kids and a Bloody Mary for herself.

She mixed up the waffle batter and got out the pan for the bacon and eggs. After plugging in the waffle iron, she was waiting for the green light to go out when she heard Nellie call, "Mom, someone's at the front door."

She unplugged the waffle iron, took off her apron, and headed for the door. When she opened it she was shocked to see David facing her.

"Hi. ..." He was stammering. "I found an earring on the floor of the car. Could you have lost one?"

She was embarrassed, standing there in her grubby t-shirt and jeans.

"Oh. ..." She stuttered. "I thought I'd lost it in the house. I couldn't find it but I was planning to search more carefully this morning."

"Well, here's your earring." He noticed how attractive she was in a t-shirt and jeans with no make-up and he noticed she was bra-less.

"I put it in this box so I wouldn't lose it. I also took the liberty to include my Uber card in case you'd like to have me as your driver when you go to the airport. My direct phone and texting number is on the back of the card."

"That's great. I'd love to have my own Uber driver, especially someone who's such a safe driver."

"If you're referring to the near miss, that was scary."

"It was. I still tremble when I think about it."

"I also included my furniture business card in the box for The House of David, the name of my business. It sounds kind of religious but I think it also suggests furniture that is well crafted."

"It's very intriguing with your name being David. Do you have a showroom? I'd love to come by and see what you have for sale."

"I have a small area in the corner of my shop that serves as a showroom. It only has a few pieces in it, partly because I don't make things fast enough and partly because when I get them finished, they seem to sell.

"I'd love to have you stop by. I'm usually there on weekends, but be sure to call first."

"I'll do that. I'm very grateful that you drove all the way here to return my earring. Can I get you a cup of coffee? That's the least I can do. I'd invite you in but I don't want the neighbors getting any ideas."

"That would be very nice. I like it black."

"Give me a minute. I'll be right back with it."

She rushed to the kitchen, put a dark roast pod in the Keurig and searched for a disposable cup. She quickly slid one under the spout just in time for the coffee to fill it. A cup of Kona coffee soon emerged.

She carried the cup carefully since it didn't have a lid. Opening the front door, she saw him standing away from it holding his cell phone, apparently taking a picture.

"Oops. I'm afraid I got a picture of you instead of the door. I love your door design and wanted it for my files."

"Let me close the door so you can get your photo." She stood to the side so he could snap the picture. While he was lining it up, he glanced briefly at her attractive braless profile, hoping she wouldn't notice.

"I got it. Thanks for the coffee. I'll be on my way now. And don't forget to call or text me if you need a ride. You have my private number." He turned and headed for his car.

She enjoyed watching his easy sway as he strolled down the path. She waited until he got in and waved.

He returned the wave and chuckled to himself about getting a photo of her without her realizing it. Just a reminder, he told himself. He pulled away from the curb and turned on his Uber phone, waiting for clients.

"Thankfully I unplugged the waffle iron," she muttered as she headed back to the kitchen, her thoughts elsewhere. He'd taken the time to drive to her house to deliver an earring. How thoughtful.

"I've got to get this breakfast back on track. But what a nice interruption."

She plugged in the waffle iron and turned on the burner for the bacon. She automatically filled the glasses with orange juice, her mind still on what had just happened.

CHAPTER 5

What luck to catch her home. She was even more attractive with her hair pulled back in a pony tail and no makeup. And the t-shirt. It was only a quick look, so he was glad he got the photo.

Later he finally decided to cancel Uber for the day and head home. When he was almost home, he stopped at a 7-11 for a candy bar, something to help settle him down.

He wondered why he was acting like a teenager? She was way above his social position. Nothing more could come of this.

He pulled into the driveway and got out his iPhone, going directly to photos. There she was, standing next to the door. Beautiful. And definitely no bra.

"Get to work David," he muttered.

The wood scent engulfed him as he entered the shop. He turned on the radio to the classical music station. Being just a carpenter, he wasn't supposed to like classical music, but the beauty and complexity of it intrigued him. Especially Bach, Mozart, and Beethoven. Although they all had different styles, they were equally wonderful to listen to.

He wanted to finish the chair. It was a special order, and the buyer was anxious to get it. He was happy with the way it was turning out, mostly made of mahogany, with alternating two-inch rows of mahogany and maple for the seat. A nice lacquer finish would complete the job. He sat on it and decided it was very comfortable.

Remaining there for a moment, he looked at his showroom located near the front door. It was separated from the rest of the shop by shower curtains to prevent sawdust from coating the finished furniture. He was proud of his various woodworking machines including saws, a drill press, a lathe, a surface planer, a jointer plane and various sanders, including two belt sanders and two disc sanders. One wall of pegboard was covered with hand tools, hanging on clasps. The other two walls had high windows that provided plenty of light. Against one of them was his desk where he could sit to sketch out plans, or just have a cup of coffee.

The picture of Melanie kept popping into his head, the attractive way she looked when she opened the door. So beautifully fresh and unassuming. How could he see her again, even for just a few moments? Maybe she'd call for an Uber ride. If so, he'd certainly cancel everything to pick her up.

He set up the sprayer and applied a coat of lacquer to the chair. Nice easy strokes back and forth so as not to cause any undesired buildup. When he finished, he removed his mask, turned on the drying lights, focused them on the chair and cleaned up the sprayer.

He walked into the kitchen and said "I'm here. We can start dinner now," He was joking of course. It wasn't his style to put himself first, especially with his family. After giving Ginny a peck on the cheek, he turned to his kids and gave them a loving squeeze.

"Hi Dad," Gary said. "The hike with the Cub Scouts was really fun. I wish you could have been with me."

"I do too, but I had a commitment of getting a piece of furniture ready for delivery tomorrow. I'm so sorry. I'll be there for sure next time."

"I understand."

"And what about you, Abby. Have you been getting into mischief?"

"Just the usual. You probably guessed that I was spending a lot of time staring at this little screen."

"I wish you wouldn't do that. Think about how you used to read a lot. That's much more stimulating."

"I know. But this is more fun."

"Enough jabbering. Take your seat David and I'll put your dinner in front of you."

"I'm ready for your famous spaghetti and meat sauce, hopefully with garlic bread."

"I made an extra amount because I know how much you like it."

They finished dinner and David got up from the table. "I have to check on the varnish to make sure it's drying properly. Did you have anything in mind for the evening?" He wanted to be in his shop.

"No. I was planning to do my e-mail and some reading."

"Okay. I'll be in the shop for a while." He had been hoping she wouldn't want to watch a movie. They didn't like the same kinds of movies but he tried to sit with her and suffer through some of them.

As he headed back to the shop his mind turned to Melanie, or should he say Mrs. Johnson? No, she introduced herself as Melanie and that's what it would be. He couldn't quit thinking about her.

CHAPTER 6

Sunday they had a nice breakfast, with David grilling the bacon on his charcoal grill. He loved the flavor when he used thick-sliced bacon and smoked it with mesquite. It was a nice morning, the sun shining brightly and the birds tweeting.

Back inside, he cooked his thin pancakes. Ginny fried eggs and made a fresh fruit salad. Sunday was a special time for the family.

After the kids left the table, he and Ginny enjoyed a second cup of coffee together. A rare event for the two of them.

"I suppose you'll be in the shop most of the day? After church, there's a ladys' luncheon and I'm on the committee, so I'll just stay after the service.

"Fine. I'm planning to start on a new table. It's going to be something special."

"You always say that about your designs. And they are always special. Maybe you'll get more customers stopping by to see what you have. The extra money would help."

"We seem to always be scraping by. I don't know what I can do to improve things. I'm always trying, but I don't know how I can spend the time to expand my business and still bring in enough money for us to survive."

"I know you are and I shouldn't nag you. Maybe I should get a job."

"Unless you could get something during the middle of the day, you shouldn't do that while the kids are at this age."

"As though they need me around. They always seem to find things to do."

"Yes, but just being here gives them stability." After helping with the dishes, he said, "I'm heading out to the shop. This new table should be worth quite a bit if it turns out the way I've planned."

The task at hand, if he could get his mind off Melanie, was to plane large pieces of blood wood, a very dense strawberry-red colored wood with golden yellow streaks, that would serve as the top of an attractive coffee table. He was sure it wouldn't last long in his showroom.

He wanted to end up with a 22-inch wide table top, but the blood wood came in 12 inch pieces. He'd plane the two 12-inch boards down to nearly the desired ¾-inch thickness and then rip each board into 4-inch strips. Gluing them together would provide the maximum stability for the table top. He'd then plane the boards down to the final desired ¾-inch thickness.

Later, before going in the house for dinner, he had time to join the six pieces, gluing elliptically-shaped wooden biscuits in slots between the boards for extra strength.

He was hungry. When he walked into the house, there was a wonderful aroma. He hoped it was her breaded pork chops with mashed potatoes, and gravy.

The four of them sat down to an attractive table setting and placed their napkins on their laps. David and Ginny worked hard to teach the kids good manners and they finally seemed to be getting it.

After dinner and dishes, Ginny said she had a good movie. David wanted to watch *60 Minutes*, his favorite TV show, but he'd record it and watch the movie. If he didn't like it, he'd go out to the shop.

CHAPTER 7

On Monday, Melanie had been thinking about David. How kind he was to take the time to deliver her earring. Not many Uber drivers would do that. They'd probably just throw the earring away. And how did he know it was hers? He must have had other women as passengers? Did he notice her that closely to remember that she was wearing pearl earrings?

She was sitting in her downtown office developing a possible TV commercial for one of her clients. It involved a new type of juicer that could do either citrus product as well as tomato juice, without having to take the skins off. Ideal subject for a TV commercial, as a special one-time offer. She knew the routine. They would take her ideas and make them into a video.

But she was having trouble concentrating. That near miss Friday weighed heavily on her mind. Another second into the intersection and she might not be around. And the way he held her hands afterwards.

She had work to do. The company wanted a presentation on Wednesday morning in New York. Wait a minute. She had her own Uber driver. Maybe she'd get to see him twice on Wednesday.

That got her back to work. It was going to be a good week.

CHAPTER 8

Tuesday night David received a phone call on his cell phone. "Hi, this is Melanie Johnson. You might not remember me, but we almost had a nasty collision with a pickup truck last Friday. You found my earring in your car and brought it to me Saturday morning. "

He was taken aback by her modesty. "I do remember you. You live on Rackleff Street."

"That's right. I need a ride to the airport early tomorrow and I was wondering if you'd be available to take me?"

"I certainly would. What time would you like me to pick you up?"

"How about 7 a.m.? I have an 8:30 flight to LaGuardia. I'll be returning later that day. A short trip this time. My return flight is scheduled to depart at 4 p.m. and I'd need a pickup at the airport but you know how flight schedules are. I'd have to text you when I'm boarding to let you know when to expect me."

"I'd be happy to pick you up."

"That's great. It will be fun having my own personal driver. It'll make me feel like an important person."

You certainly are, he thought.

■ ■ ■

Wednesday he was up at 5:30, a little earlier than usual. He couldn't sleep. Too excited about seeing Melanie. Why was that?

He felt like a kid on Christmas morning.

Settle down. It's just another passenger. But no it wasn't. He made sure he was wearing his new black jeans and a nice shirt.

Moving into the kitchen, he could see that Ginny had set out a bagel for him, and a note said there was cream cheese in the fridge. For Ginny's sake he gulped down his multi-vitamin with a glass of juice.

Then out the back door and into his shop to get the small vase and scissors to cut some flowers. He remembered she'd commented about them when she got into the car. Probably a mixture of roses would look good, some red, some yellow. After picking them and putting the vase in the dash holder, he was off to Rackleff Street. He thought of stopping for a cup of coffee but decided to wait until after he'd dropped her off.

It wasn't long before he pulled up in front of her house. He hadn't remembered the number but he recognized the one with the carved wood front door. He got out of his car and headed up the walkway. Just as he began to climb the steps, the door opened and there she was, as beautiful as ever. She wore a dark blue suit, with a blue and white scarf around her neck and her hair in a bun.

"Hi...Melanie?" He hadn't forgotten her name, but it had escaped him for a moment.

"Hi. It's good to see you again," she said. He looked very attractive, wearing nice jeans and a dark blue long-sleeved work-type shirt. And his hair was mostly combed but it had a bit of a tousled look, which she liked.

"Since it's a day trip, I assume you don't have any luggage?"

"Just my leather portfolio case. But I do have a favor to ask. I'll tell you when we get in the car."

"That works for me." He opened the back door and she slid in. Darn, no skirt this time. He slid into the driver's side and pulled away from the curb.

"So what's the favor?"

"I forgot to bring two of my sketches with me and didn't realize it until about an hour ago. Could we stop at my downtown office on the way to the airport? I could run in and grab them and be right out. It wouldn't take long."

"My time is your time. You're the one who has to catch a plane, so whatever you want to do is fine with me. Where's your office?"

"It's on Congress Street in the 400 block."

"What a coincidence. There's a Starbucks on Congress, and I stop there almost every Friday around 10 a.m. for a tall mocha. That's my splurge for the week. They make the best mochas."

"I know where that is. It's just a few blocks from my office. I never go there since I don't have anyone to go with and it's a fairly long walk for a coffee. I usually go to a small place near my office."

"If you're looking for someone to have coffee with, you know when I'm usually there. I didn't quite mean it the way it sounded. I just thought if you happened to come by when I was there, we could chat for a few minutes."

"What if someone I knew saw me sitting there talking with another man?"

"I know what you mean. But I always sit at the counter, not a table, which would make it less risky. And there's usually a stool available next to me. You could sit there and we could pretend we didn't know each other. I'm not even suggesting we meet. I'm just rambling."

"That's alright. I do that sometimes."

When they came to Congress Street, she pointed to her building. "That's it across the street. The one with the red doors. I can see that there's no parking available but if you let me out and drive around the block, I should be out by the time you return. But drive slowly."

"And if you're not here, I'll drive around again, so don't rush."

"I think I can make it quick."

The first drive around, no Melanie. But when he approached the second time, she was waiting at the curb wearing a broad smile. A chill went down his spine when he saw her.

He pulled up and she jumped in.

"Were you able to get what you needed?"

"I did and I thank you again for doing this. I know the extra gas adds to your cost so I'll give you an extra tip."

"Are you kidding? The extra gas might be a few cents. Don't worry about it. We at Uber aim to please."

"I just want you to know how much I appreciate your doing this diversion."

"So, it's off to the Jetport."

"And I have plenty of time to make my flight."

They pulled up to the terminal and he got out quickly to open her door. She was still getting her portfolio so he got there in time to offer his hand. Not that she needed it, but he was hoping to briefly hold hers.

"Oh, a gentleman again. I thank you for your service."

She was uncomfortably aware of that brief moment when their hands were touching.

"I remember your instructions. You'll text when you're boarding the plane at LaGuardia and I'll be able to track your flight on my iPhone. Have a good flight."

She began walking towards the terminal and quickly turned around.

"I completely forgot about the tip. Here is something extra for picking me up, being my own personal driver, and stopping to get my sketches." She handed him a five-dollar bill, their hands brushing briefly.

"You don't have to do that since the tip is built into the charge but thanks very much. I'll see you later today."

He got into his car and pulled away from the curb.

What was so magic about touching her hand? That was the third time it happened and each time it sent a chill down his back.

He had a difficult time concentrating while heading for his construction site. Too many thoughts. He'd advised his boss that he'd be a little late. He was such a skilled employee, his boss didn't mind if he took an extra privilege now and then.

CHAPTER 9

Did their hands touch more than they normally would for someone helping her out of the car? That happened so seldom that she almost didn't remember what it was like. There was something about him that made it special. Some kind of a connection.

She got in the long TSA screening line, listening to passengers complaining about not being able to take their water bottle with them, or having to take their shoes off, or other issues. In contrast, most of the screeners were very pleasant and helpful.

After being cleared, she headed for her gate. It was a clean airport, not too crowded, unlike the airports at bigger cities, such as LaGuardia. The company she consulted with paid for her to fly first class, which she loved. During the boarding process, after she was settled in her seat, she watched most of the passengers head to the rear to be packed in like sardines.

She hoped her presentation would go well. She'd been working on the idea for over a month and this was her first chance to present it to the marketing manager. Then he would take her to lunch and afterwards discuss her presentation. She wondered where they would go, not that she knew the New York restaurant scene that well.

After a short flight and a smooth landing, she headed out of the terminal, texted for an Uber and within about two minutes a driver pulled up.

There it was, a white Prius. The driver must want to keep his expenses down. She approached, verified the type of car and license plate and moved to the rear door. After opening it, the driver turned to her and said "Mrs. Johnson? Melanie."

"That's me, so I guess I'm in the right place." She climbed in and directed him to Manhattan at 46th Street and 8th Avenue. When they arrived, she handed him a two-dollar tip. No opening of her door. Instead, just, "Here we are."

She got out and headed for her building with offices on the 5th floor.

Her presentation went better than she expected. Afterward, the group suggested lunch at Barbetta, which turned out to be an elegant Northern Italian trattoria with an upscale menu and a very substantial wine list.

They were seated in a nice garden-style patio area surrounded by beautiful flowers. She learned it was one of the oldest restaurants in Manhattan, opening in 1906. She concluded that she was being treated extra well for giving a favorable presentation.

After a tasty pasta dish and salad, and a glass of White Burgundy, she finished with a delicious crème bruleé, the caramelized topping made perfectly.

The afternoon critique went well. They loved her ideas and said they were going to pursue them. They'd have her return later to critique the final commercial.

Then another Uber back to the airport. Her thoughts turned to David, as they seemed to frequently. She remembered she said she would text him, but decided she'd phone instead.

She boarded the plane and settled into a comfortable window seat, deciding to have a drink before take-off.

"May I help you?"

"Yes, I'd love a glass of red wine. What are you serving today?"

"We have a Cabernet Sauvignon and a Syrah, both from the Napa Valley."

"I'd like a glass of the Syrah please. And a snack of some kind."

"I'll be right back with that."

The wine came and she had a few sips while watching the unlucky passengers heading for the rear.

After finishing the wine, she settled in her seat, hoping for a smooth flight. Within a short time, she leaned her head against the window and fell asleep.

■ ■ ■

"Please put your seat backs up and make sure your seat belts are fastened, We will be landing soon," came the loud announcement.

She responded with a jerk and realized she'd been sleeping. They were almost there. Why was she so excited about that? Heading home and having to cook dinner. Then she remembered she also need to text David when she arrived.

CHAPTER 10

He kept looking at his watch, hoping the afternoon would pass quickly. At 4:10 his phone rang.

"Hi. This is Melanie Johnson calling from the airport in New York., instead of texting. Is this my Uber driver?"

"You've reached the right person. What can I do for you today? Just joking. I assume you're about to board your flight. I have the flight number and I'll be at the airport to pick you up. I'll be waiting at the cell phone parking lot so give me a call or text me when you get off the plane."

"Sounds great. See you soon."

Did she sound excited about seeing him? Oh, didn't he wish. Her flight took about an hour and a half so he should be seeing her around 5:45.

• • •

It was 5:42 when his phone rang. "Hello, this is Uber." He assumed it was Melanie.

"I hope it's my Uber or should I say David," she said laughingly. "I'm here."

"It is indeed and I'm waiting for you. I could say 'anxiously' waiting but that would be inappropriate."

"Not at all. I'm looking forward to seeing you. I'll be at the curb in a few minutes."

"My engine is running and I'm on my way."

When he pulled up to the curb, he didn't see her.

He could always go around again if the airport police signaled him. Then he saw her moving along slowly, looking in both directions, as beautiful as ever.

Waving to him, she got in the back seat and closed the door.

"I assume you want to go home?"

She had a questioning look.

"I mean, …you don't need to stop at your office?"

"Oh, no, I don't need to stop there. But to answer your other question, I wouldn't mind taking a long route home to be able to unwind. But I have to cook dinner, so I need to get there sooner than later."

"I was hoping to hear about your trip, as if it would make any sense to me. So Rackleff Avenue, here we come."

"I can tell you it went very well. They were so impressed they took me to one of the oldest and best restaurants in New York for lunch. It's nice to have something you've worked on get appreciated."

"You're right."

"But you have that happen with your furniture."

"Yes, that does happen, but not often enough. I mean, I don't have the time to produce as much as I'd like to so I don't get much feedback."

But I'll bet your furniture is of really high quality."

"Why don't you stop by sometime and see for yourself."

"I should do that."

They were soon pulling up to her house.

He jumped out and went to her side of the car, quickly pulling the door open.

"That's right. I get to have the royal treatment. Thank you, sir."

"My pleasure." He held out his hand and helped her out of the car.

"I'll be calling you for my next trip, but I'm not sure when that will be." She hesitated and then offered her hand again, not knowing whether that was appropriate, but she wanted to do it. "Thanks for the special attention. Having my own personal driver is fun."

She turned and walked to the front door.

David climbed in and pulled away from the curb. He'd wanted to stand there and wave goodbye but decided not to. He did notice that she turned and looked at him before going inside.

And she'd also called him by name when she phoned.

CHAPTER 11

Entering the house, she paused in the hall. Why was it so exciting to take an Uber? It was David, of course. And why did she offer her hand before she headed for the front door? That was not what you do with taxi drivers. But it was something she wanted to do. Making that small connection felt good.

"Hi Zelda. I'm home."

The white kitchen door opened and Zelda's head appeared. "That's great! You made it safely. I can relax now. With all of these airline crashes lately, I worry about you when you're traveling."

"Oh, Zelda, It's much safer than going somewhere in a car."

"But at least you're not stranded at 30,000 feet, or landing at 150 miles an hour."

"The statistics show it to be very safe."

"I'll remember that. I bought some pork chops you can fry and I made potato salad. I knew you'd probably be late."

"That's so sweet of you. I appreciate that very much." She gave her a hug and headed upstairs to change.

Getting out of her business suit, she was in the process of putting on jeans and a t-shirt when she glanced at the mirror, wearing only her bra and panties. Not bad for a 35-year old. Her breasts were full and her stomach was flat. She was careful about how much she ate and she visited the gym on a regular basis.

She always looked forward to being in her bright and cheerful kitchen. Opening the fridge door, she could see the delicious-looking potato salad. Also the thin pork chops would be good breaded and fried. A green salad would go well with them even though the kids wouldn't eat much of it.

As she was pouring a glass of white wine Paul walked through the door, his tie loose and his jacket unbuttoned. "Hi sweetheart. How was your trip? A short one this time. You must have wowed them." He gave her the usual peck on the cheek.

"I didn't wow them but they loved what I proposed. They even took me to an upscale restaurant for lunch. I was pleased with how everything went." Including getting to see David twice in one day, she thought.

"Zelda left potato salad and I'll fry some pork chops. Get into your evening duds and have your scotch and soda. By that time dinner will be ready."

"You treat me too well sometimes."

"That's because I love you," she said, wondering if their relationship was really love anymore. More like friends. They had sex once in a while but far less often than they used to. What would it be like to have a passionate relationship at this time in her life? With Paul or maybe someone else?

■ ■ ■

David drove home, not paying much attention to his driving. His thoughts were elsewhere. After pulling into the driveway, he went to his shop to make sure his gluing of the table top turned out okay. Removing the clamps, he picked up the large rectangular piece of wood and admired it, imagining how great it would look when finished. Then he ambled into the house.

It was almost 6:30, but Ginny was used to that. She knew how important their Uber income was.

When he walked in, the dinner aromas greeted him. He could see the baked lasagna on the stove. He had given Ginny a rough estimate of when he'd arrive, and it looked like the lasagna had just come out of the oven. His mouth began to water. A bottle of red wine was on the table with the cork removed. They didn't often drink wine. Too expensive. But it was special to have it with an Italian meal.

"You're just in time. Dinner's ready. I'll call the kids and we can have our salad."

After washing up, he returned to the table and they were soon seated.

Gary spoke first. "Dad, we won our game today. And I got two base hits. One was a double."

"That's great! I'm sorry I couldn't make it. I had passengers to pick up."

Abby smiled and said, "I just wanted you to know that I got an A on my English paper. It was about a girl and her dog. I wish we could have one."

"You know your mother's view about dogs. She thinks she's allergic to them. So I don't think we'll be getting one any time soon."

"I know. I guess I'll just have to write about them."

"You know honey, I'd love for you to have a dog, but then I might have to move out."

"I know Mom."

The conversation was about pets for the rest of the meal.

"Abby and Gary, you two clean off the table and load the dishwasher and I'll do the final cleanup. Dad will most likely go to his shop."

Exactly what he'd planned. Now he had permission without asking.

When he entered the shop, he sensed the freedom. His thoughts turned to Melanie and how she took his hand to thank him. Did that mean anything? Where could this be going?

CHAPTER 12

Melanie arrived at her office on Friday morning expecting to have her usual unexciting day, spending most of the time working on a new assignment. She glanced up at the large clock above her desk and saw that it was 9:30. Suddenly she thought of David. He said he usually visited the Starbucks around ten on Fridays. Could she wander down there and casually bump into him? But she told him she'd never been there before. She could say that she wanted to see what Starbucks was like and decided to check it out.

She put away her sketches and headed for the door. It was about a ten to fifteen-minute walk. Five short blocks.

During her walk along the colorful brick sidewalk, she was attracted to the displays in the windows of a women's store. She saw a rust-colored shawl that would be a nice addition to her wardrobe. Maybe she should stop on the way back to the office.

When she reached Starbucks, she looked through the window and couldn't see David, so she headed inside. Getting in line would make it look like she hadn't come to meet someone. No David. Could he be in the restroom?

"May I help you?"

"Uh, yes. I'd just like a cup of coffee."

"What size, Tall or Grande?

"I don't know what you mean."

"Tall is our smallest cup. Starbucks jargon. I guess you haven't been here before. But we aim to please. So why don't you take a Tall to see if you like our coffee. When you come next time, you'll know the routine."

"That sounds great. I'll have a Tall one." Looking around, still no David.

She paid for her coffee and moved to the station where she picked it up. She'd drink it on the way back to the office. A real disappointment.

. . .

I guess I won't make it to Starbucks today. Putting up these trusses requires two people, so I can't leave. And I have to be extra careful that one of them doesn't fall on me again. If Melanie shows up at the Starbucks and I'm not there, I hope she'll try again next Friday.

. . .

During the next week, David was busy with his usual construction jobs, driving Uber when he had time, and slipping into his shop on a few evenings. When Friday arrived, he arranged his work so that he could take his morning break, leaving for Starbucks about 9:30. He wanted to be there first, if she showed up.

. . .

Melanie was busy that week, developing ideas for her new project. She typically spent 8:30 a.m. to 3 p.m. in her downtown office. It was 9:30 when she looked up at the clock. What was at 10:00? How could she forget? It's Friday. David's day at Starbucks. She'd try again. The coffee was good, but was it worth the five-block walk? It certainly would be if David were there. She decided to give it one more try.

She strolled down Congress Street, watching the people passing by, wondering where they were headed. Another attractive window display in the boutique made her pause and gaze at the clothing. When she arrived at Starbucks she looked in the window. Her mouth began to water when she saw the attractive dessert display cases.

There he was, sitting at one of the shiny wood counters on a high stool. He was facing away from the window, his head cocked to the side as though he was reading something. And a stool next to him was vacant.

He'd told her he liked Starbuck's mochas so she decided to try one and carry it to the counter and surprise him.

She got in the ordering line and when her turn came she asked for a Grande low-fat mocha. She was proud that she'd remembered the terminology.

She stood around until they called out," One low fat Grande mocha."

"Thanks," she said as they handed it to her.

She turned and quietly approached David on his right. "Pardon me. Is this seat taken?"

"Melanie!" Then a quick whisper, "Oh, I'm not supposed to know you.

"No. It's not. Please have a seat."

"Thank you. The place is crowded this morning. All the tables are full."

"It usually is on Friday mornings."

"I came last Friday and it wasn't this crowded. But I didn't stay."

David got out his cell phone and pretended to be talking, keeping his voice down. "I'm so glad you took the time to come again. I'm sorry I wasn't here last week, but I'm very honored, that is if I'm the reason you came."

"I shouldn't admit it, but I guess it is. I'm curious to know more about you."

"My life's not that interesting. But I keep busy."

"It sounds interesting to me."

"That gives me an idea of how you could get to know me better. You might think I'm a little forward but would you consider having lunch with me sometime? It certainly wouldn't be a date. Just a chance to get to know each other better."

"You're catching me off guard. I've only had lunch with a man, other than my husband, at a business lunch."

"We could think of this as a business lunch. Uber business."

"But how could we do it without risk of being discovered? I'm not sure what the implications of this are. I certainly wouldn't want my husband to find out."

"And I wouldn't want Ginny to be aware of it either. But people get together for lunch all the time without any serious thoughts about it. If we just happened to meet at Starbucks at noon someday and I was sitting here having a sandwich and you walked in, I'd certainly offer you a place at the table while you ate your sandwich."

"You're right. I guess it's the idea of secretly going away somewhere that bothers me."

"I guess it does me too. I'm just thinking as we talk, but we could go somewhere away from Portland. I've seen a seafood restaurant in a small town overlooking Casco Bay where probably no one goes except the locals. The reason I know about it is that I've been out there on a few Uber runs and have always wanted to try the place.

What was it about him that was drawing her to him? Perhaps it was the feeling of missing something in her life. A mid-life crisis? But it was more than that. She felt a special closeness to him.

"Tell me more. How would we get there? I'm assuming this would be on a business day, a business lunch as you call it."

"You wouldn't want to get into my car around here, even though it has an Uber sticker. Maybe you could take the bus to a place where we could meet, so you wouldn't have to be seen driving. And your car still being parked near your office would make people think you were still there. I know that sounds pretty secretive but I think I know the ideal place to meet. The

CVS Pharmacy out on Congress Street

"I know your tricks. You've got me thinking about how to do this, instead of if we should do it at all."

"I'm really not that clever. But I think it would be fun."

"I do too. I guess it can't hurt. We're just attempting to get better acquainted since you're my regular driver and we'd have more to talk about when you take me to the airport."

"Let's get down to some details. How about meeting next Wednesday at 12 noon at the CVS Pharmacy? It's very near the intersection of Congress Street and Stevens Avenue at the Westgate Shopping Center, near where the bus stops."

"Are you sure you haven't been planning this."

"Absolutely not. I'm very impressed that you would even consider me capable of doing that," he said, laughing. "The reason I know my way around town is because I'm an Uber driver."

"So it's Wednesday at noon. Let's meet inside the pharmacy. That way I can be browsing among the cosmetics until you arrive."

"Unless I arrive first. And in case of an emergency and one of us can't show up, we'll plan do it again the next week."

She looked directly at him for the first time and risked a smile. "I like adventures. See you Wednesday. And by the way, I love mochas." She got up and left.

He continued to pretend to talk on his cell phone for another few minutes, then left.

What was happening? He had a lunch date with another woman. A woman very much above his social status. Why would she be interested in him? Was this for real?

CHAPTER 13

He returned to his SUV, climbed in and sat for a moment, stunned. He had arranged a date with a beautiful woman. Was he cheating on Ginny? He decided things hadn't gone far enough to consider it cheating. Just lunch.

Driving back to the construction site, he was lost in thought. He would have trouble concentrating during the rest of the day. Fortunately he had some window framing that could be done without thinking.

Later, when he arrived home, wonderful smells were permeating the kitchen. Ginny was busy at the stove stirring something, and he leaned over and gave her a kiss on the lips. Usually it was just a peck on the cheek, but he did this to assuage his guilty feelings. She put her arms around his neck and returned the kiss.

He could see that she'd made Coq au Vin, a favorite of his. While he was leaning over the pot, sniffing, she poured him a glass of Chardonnay. Did she suspect something? He wasn't used to having wine with dinner, but it was Friday. Maybe that was her excuse.

"What's with the fancy dinner? It smells good. And wine to go with it."

"Oh, I just felt like making something nice for you. I know you work hard to feed our family and I don't express my appreciation often enough."

"Yes you do, and I can assure you the dinner will be very

much appreciated." But why the affection this night?

Later, in the shop, he had to be extra careful not to hurt himself since he didn't have his usual concentration.

■ ■ ■

Melanie walked slowly to her office, stopping briefly at the boutique but not paying much attention to the clothes in the window. She was experiencing new feelings. Fascination with David, but also the excitement that she shouldn't be doing what she was doing. It was partially that, but also some anger with herself for doing something that wasn't right. But her thoughts about David were there. She couldn't help it.

Back at the office, her work moved slowly, continually interrupted by thoughts of David. They hadn't touched hands but just being close felt very comfortable.

And then he proposed having lunch with her! That was surprising. And more surprising was that she accepted. What was she thinking? It was a date! No question about it. She was married and had made a date with a married man. With that thought in mind, she got very little done.

Later, arriving home, she felt guilty and went around the house picking things up, straightening the rugs, using the hand vacuum to collect crumbs off the kitchen floor, anything to keep her mind off of Starbucks.

When Paul walked through the door, she gave him a kiss on the lips, unusual for her at this time of day.

"Wow. Where did that come from?"

"I was just thinking about you and wanted you to know it."

She heated up Zelda's casserole and put together a salad. Garlic bread helped satisfy the kids and ice cream was a welcomed dessert.

When dinner was over, they went their separate ways, the kids to homework and video games, Paul to the TV in the family room, and she to her hideaway. At that point Starbucks was still very much on her mind.

. . .

It wasn't long before Wednesday came around, although it seemed like an eternity to both David and Melanie.

David had his normal breakfast routine of granola, toast, and juice.

"Can I make you a cup of coffee?" Ginny said.

"That would be great. And could you put it in my thermos?"

"So is it your usual carpentering today or will you be doing Uber?"

That caught him off guard. "I'll be carpentering this morning but not sure what I'll be doing this afternoon. It depends on how far along we get with the house." Funny, she didn't often ask about his plans during the day. Had he been acting different lately?

He was out the door and off to his job. He purposely finished a small project. He'd tell his boss he had some plans for lunch and wouldn't be back until mid-afternoon.

"Oh, something special going on?" he said, looking at him slyly.

"No. Just meeting an old friend from high school."

"OK, I've got a new project I'll get you started on when you get back."

When 11:30 rolled around he cleaned up his wood scraps and sawdust, put away his tools, and headed for the car. He knew it wouldn't take more than 15 minutes to get to the mall, but he wanted to be there early to check things out. He found a good parking spot close to the pharmacy entrance.

. . .

Melanie awakened, excited. She jumped out of bed and noticed that Paul had already gone downstairs. She took an extra-long shower, carefully washing her hair. While dressing, she spent time choosing the right outfit. She wanted to wear something casual, but not too casual since she'd be at work for a good part of the day. She chose some black jeans along with a cream colored long-sleeve silk blouse, with only the top unbuttoned. Low-heeled sandals completed her outfit. She tied her hair in a ponytail, holding it with an attractive brown plastic clip. Normal for the office.

When she got to the kitchen, Paul had finished his breakfast and was heading out the door. "You look especially nice today. Anything going on at the office?"

"No. I guess sometimes women like to change their appearance for no special reason. I just wanted to look nice for you." She lied.

"Well, you certainly do. That gets me off to a good start. Bye now." He gave her a peck on the cheek and was out the door.

She poured Raisin Bran for the kids and fixed toast with strawberry jam, a breakfast they loved. When they finished, they were off to the school bus stop, leaving her alone. She felt somewhat out of control.

Gathering her things together, she headed for the car and was soon entering her building. She took the stairs two at a time, working off some nervous energy. When 11:30 rolled around, she headed out the door and hurried to the bus stop, not that she had to rush.

When the bright blue Congress Street bus pulled up, she boarded and was greeted by the friendly bus driver as she paid her fare.

She found a seat near the front so she could watch for the CVS Pharmacy at the Westgate Shopping Center. When it finally came into view, she pushed the stop button and prepared to get off. What was she getting into?

CHAPTER 14

David arrived 10 minutes early, wandered around the parking lot for a few minutes and then went into CVS. He found the men's toiletries and began browsing, keeping an eye on the store entrance. He thought his pulse and blood pressure must be increasing.

There she was, looking around rather sheepishly and then slowly meandering to the women's cosmetics. He decided to head for the front door, passing her on the way. He whispered to meet him at his car around the corner of the building. She made an inconspicuous nod and watch him hasten out the door.

Once inside his car, he sat for a moment, realizing how uncomfortable the situation was. Too late to back out.

He drove over to the side of the store and watched as she came around the corner, climbing into the back seat.

"Hi. I thought I should pretend to be an Uber passenger until we get out of the mall. Would I be allowed to move up front with you later?"

"If you didn't move up, I'd have to drop you off somewhere, as I do other passengers." It was small talk. When they approached the main highway, he pulled over to the side of the road

"Time to move up."

"We sat close at Starbucks, but not like this. Kind of scary."

They were quiet for a while. Than Melanie finally spoke. "I'm anxious to see where we're going. It sounds charming. You said not many people, other than locals, know about it."

"I've taken a passenger to that area several times and he always tells me the restaurant is relatively unknown in Portland, but for me to be sure to try it."

"I'm in the mood for seafood, probably scallops. I guess I should get lobster but we often have that when the price is low, so scallops move to the top of the list." She was trying to make small talk.

"I love scallops but we don't have lobster very often. Too expensive and the kids aren't used to it. I think a lobster roll will work for me, if they have it."

They drove along for a while without talking, feeling a little nervous. Finally they began to anticipate their destination.

"This area is not built up with a lot of tourist restaurants, motels, or stores. I like the feeling."

"So do I."

"I'm surprised such an area exists this close to Portland."

"Yes, I think of that every time I bring my passenger here. And you're definitely not my passenger today. I don't know what I'd refer to you as, but maybe my guest."

"But we're going Dutch treat for lunch. That way I won't have to think of it as a date."

"If that's what you wish, that's what we'll do."

CHAPTER 15

When they arrived, she saw a charming old cottage surrounded by struggling shrubs. A screen door on the front had a weathered look. A few old tables on an adjacent patio were surrounded by a white picket fence with the paint peeling off and partially covered with vines. Some of the available parking spots were in the rear, which pleased Melanie.

David parked and jumped out hoping to open Melanie's door. Too bad no skirt but that wasn't important. Being with her was all that mattered.

"Let's find a table away from the front door where it's private," David said.

"You lead the way."

"How about the one in the far corner. No one is seated near it. In fact, very few people are here today."

"I love the place. It looks so inviting with the nice tablecloths and flowers."

As he pulled her chair out, he noticed she sat down in a very relaxed way. Not abrupt like some people might. He admired her beauty while he was sitting down. It wasn't that of a movie star, but more a simple, refreshing look. She wore very little makeup. She certainly didn't need any. And this was the second time he'd seen her with an attractive ponytail. Her brown eyes and narrow face with high cheekbones made her look perfect.

While David was seating her, she managed a glimpse at him.

His warm tenderness and thoughtfulness were very apparent. His rugged look was quite sexy, although she didn't want to admit it.

They sat for a few minutes, sometimes looking at each other and sometimes looking away. The server approached and asked if she could get them something to drink.

They looked at each other and Melanie said, "Maybe a glass of white wine, possibly a Chardonnay. Something inexpensive. I usually don't drink wine for lunch, but I think I'd like a glass today."

"I'll have what she's having," David replied. They broke into laughter, remembering the famous line from the movie.

"I hardly ever drink wine. On a carpenter's budget, we can't afford it. But I do have a beer occasionally, particularly on weekends. Also, I don't dare drink when I'll be working in the shop. I could lose a finger."

"I can imagine you have to be very careful. I'd love to see your shop sometime, or your showroom. You gave me your card and said you were there on weekends. Could I give you a call and stop by sometime?"

"I'd love that. Call first to make sure I'm there. The number on my business card is not my Uber phone number. It's our regular house phone but the answering message is for my furniture business, The House of David. It's all on the card I gave you."

"I still have it."

The server soon placed their wine on the table. Melanie picked hers up and held it toward David. "Let's click glasses and toast to a skillful Uber driver who's my hero."

"Thank you." He picked up his glass and clicked hers.

"I wish I knew what I was doing here," Melanie said.

"Me too. I have to admit, mostly to myself but also to you, that I feel like you're a magnet, pulling me towards you. It feels like an addiction."

"I feel something similar."

"I don't see a clear pathway ahead. But I'm just happy to be here."

"Live in the moment, some famous person once said."

The server approached and they ordered.

"I'll have the scallops with linguine, and a small Caesar salad to begin with."

"That's great. And you sir?"

" I'd like the lobster roll, and I'll also have a Caesar salad to start."

"The regular size, not the small one?"

"Yes. And we'd like to have separate checks."

That's fine. I'll get these orders right in."

"Maybe we should know a little more about each other. Why don't you tell me where you grew up and what got you into being a carpenter, as well as designing and making fine furniture."

"It's not very interesting. I grew up in a little town north of here called Lisbon Falls. It was known for its wood products. And I guess I'm actually a product of wood, in that my life is devoted to wood in one way or another. After high school, I got a job as a carpenter's apprentice and here I am."

"I'm sure there's a lot more to it than that. Being a carpenter doesn't make you a designer and builder of artistic furniture."

"You're right. My family didn't have enough money to send me to college. But I took some night classes in woodworking and design at the community college in Portland. I did well and that launched my other career."

"A person would never know that you don't have a college education."

"I only attended a few night classes, as I mentioned, but I read a lot."

"That's obvious."

"And by the way, Stephen King grew up and went to high school in Lisbon Falls, obviously before my time. Someone who has written nearly 60 novels has to be a bit older than I am. I've read a few of his books but I don't care for his science fiction style. I prefer more realistic thrillers such as those written by John Grisham or David Baldacci. I read one or two books a week, mainly at night while getting myself sleepy enough to turn out the lamp. My wife has learned to go to sleep with my bedside light on."

"What about your family?"

"I thought your question was just about me. But my family is certainly a big part of me. Ginny and I fell in love in high school and got married shortly thereafter. She was head cheer leader and I was offered a scholarship to play on a college team but couldn't manage to go. We thought we were the perfect couple. Maybe we were at that point in our lives."

"I can just picture you back then. A prize catch for some lucky girl."

"I wouldn't say that. But shortly after we were married our delightful daughter Abby came along, and two years later, Gary. He's a baseball fan, and Abby loves to dance. They're beautiful kids. As far as our marriage goes, it's sort of moving along in the way it's supposed to after the initial romance: she going her way and I going mine. Until I met you. Now I don't know what's happening."

There was a long pause.

"What about you? How did you get to the point of being a successful graphic designer."

"I'd love to tell you but here comes our lunch. Why don't we continue after we finish eating?"

"Sounds good."

CHAPTER 16

The server placed their salads on the table and asked if there was anything else she could bring them?

"I'd like some Parmesan cheese grated on top of mine."

"The same for me," Melanie said.

"I don't know about your salad but mine is very good. The romaine is fresh and crisp, and I taste the garlic in the croutons."

"How does a carpenter know so much about the specific ingredients of a Caesar salad," she said laughingly?"

"I love food and I love to cook. So do we have time to start on you?"

"Sure. I grew up here in Portland, was very interested in art and design in high school and won a scholarship to the Rhode Island School of Design or RISD as they call it. It was there that I discovered my talent in graphic design and obtained a Bachelor's Degree. I spent two years at a well-known advertising agency in New York City but I missed Maine so much that I decided to try working here on my own. I made enough contacts while in New York that I was able to survive, but just barely. I guess I was good enough that my business finally built up to where I can now be a little choosy about what jobs I take on."

"That's great. But what about your family?"

"I met Paul when I got back to Portland. It was at a friend's party and we hit it off and were married a year later. I didn't realize at the time that he was such a sports fanatic or should I say addict. He watches every type of game on TV and I wouldn't be surprised if he bets on some of them."

"Any children?"

"We have two kids, Nellie aged 13 and Josh aged 12. Nellie loves to draw and paint. She must take after me, and Josh is a sports nut, continually watching games with his Dad. Paul's game-watching doesn't leave much time for the two of us."

"I can imagine that it wouldn't."

"Paul is an accountant and his friends are too. And they're also sports buffs. Accounting is a pretty boring subject for me, but he seems to like it. And between the two of us we do well financially, so I guess I can't complain."

"Thanks for sharing that. It looks like the rest of our lunch is coming."

"You mean that's all I have to say? Saved by the bell."

"There's more? I'd love to hear it."

"Maybe after we eat."

Their food was delicious.

"This lobster roll is great. I think there's meat of more than one lobster in it. And the coleslaw is also good."

"My scallops are cooked perfectly, crisp on the outside and tender in the middle. And I love the linguini. You did good in finding this place. What's the name of it?"

"Their sign needs some work but I think it's called Bob's Lobster Shack. They don't advertise much so you wouldn't have heard of it. I think they mostly depend on word of mouth, and the locals."

"I won't spread the word around. I wouldn't want it to get well known in Portland. If that happened, it might get difficult to get a reservation."

"You said 'saved by the bell'. What were you saved from?"

"I guess it's just the fact that I'm getting a bit bored with what I'm doing. Same old routine even though each project is different. And at home, it's fix dinner and then off to my office, with Paul watching sports and the kids texting."

"What does that mean?"

I don't know where it's going, but I'll be honest. I'm having trouble getting you out of my mind. I realize that it's risky telling you that. We hardly know each other, so maybe I shouldn't be revealing my feelings."

"I couldn't have said it better. That's exactly what's been happening to me."

"What do we do about it?"

"I have no idea except that I'd love to have lunch like this with you again sometime. Do you think we could do that, and maybe soon? I'd be devastated if we can't. It's the only way I can think of to be with you, except for the brief moments at Starbucks when we can't really talk very much or when you hire me to Uber you."

"That's an interesting verb: Uber."

"I just made it up."

The server put their individual checks in front of them and they paid with cash, thinking they didn't want a record of the lunch.

Getting up from the table, they headed out the rear door to the car, David following closely behind Melanie. When he opened her car door, he grasped her hand and reached around for the other one, holding them briefly while they looked at each other.

"Thank you for coming. I've loved this time together."

"Me too." They both wanted to hug but held back, thinking it might go too far.

When they arrived back at the mall, he let her off next to the pharmacy. She jumped out quickly, waved goodbye and surprised herself by blowing him a kiss.

CHAPTER 17

David walked around to his side of the car, unlocked the door and slid quickly into his seat. He sat there for a few minutes, staring straight ahead at the peeling paint on the side of the building. What an amazing experience he just had! It was probably one of the most significant events of his life. He suddenly realized they had made no special plans to meet again. The only chance was if she showed up at Starbucks on Friday. He'd make sure he was there.

How could he go back to pounding nails? But he had to since he told his boss he'd be there, and for that matter, what else would he do?

She was more than he'd imagined. So intriguing and thoughtful. And she admitted she felt the same about him. She had even blown him a kiss! The memory of that gesture would certainly last for a while.

While driving next to the picturesque waterways on this beautiful sunny day, he hardly noticed the colorful boats. His focus was primarily on Melanie. He could not imagine any possible pathway for them to be together.

When he got back to the job site, his boss approached, ready to give him his afternoon project. "You look a little down. Anything wrong? Anything happen at lunch?"

"No, just an old high-school friend suffering with some problems," actually referring to himself.

"I've got a simple job for you. The owner requested moving the framing of this closet to the other side of the room. Why can't they make up their mind? I get more money when they make these changes, but it slows things down. I've got the new location marked on the floor."

"Thanks. I'll get right to it." Something to get his mind off of Melanie.

. . .

Melanie saw the blue bus approaching, ready to take her back to the real world. After stepping on and paying her fare, she proceeded to the rear and found a comfortable seat near a window, wanting to be alone. Too many feelings to sort out. She'd wanted to give him a hug when they departed but didn't dare.

Watching for her stop was difficult since she was having trouble concentrating. Returning to work didn't appeal to her, but she didn't know what else to do. Maybe stopping at Starbucks would help. She'd get a mocha to remind her of him.

Seeing Starbucks ahead, she pressed the buzzer and got off. Arriving at the counter she said, "A low fat mocha Grande, please." She now knew the jargon.

When they called out her drink, she took it over to the counter where they'd sat together, and began sipping it while remembering the last time she was there. Feeling a little better, she hoped she could make it through the rest of the day.

It was an afternoon of useless energy. Nothing seemed to work. Layouts she made didn't coordinate with each other. A wasted effort. It was finally time to head home, but to what? Fix dinner for the family and then up to her hideaway?

After dinner, she decided to take a walk. She could try to appreciate the night air, the clear sky, the stars. She wasn't in a hurry. Getting back to the house soon was not part of her plan.

It was quiet outside. Very few cars. Although difficult to see, the violet rhododendron and yellow pittosporum were blooming in all their splendor. After walking for about an hour, she realized she was almost home. They had a nice house, but it didn't look very inviting. But what else was there to do? She went in and called out "I'm home!"

"Where have you been?" exclaimed Paul as he approached her. "I was worried when I went up to your office and you weren't there."

"I yelled out when I left that I was going out for a walk. You were probably too engrossed in your game to hear me."

"I didn't hear you. What did you do?"

"I just went for a long walk to burn off some nervous energy. It was a tough day at work." Truer words were never spoken.

"You can go back to your game. I'll see you later in bed."

She went upstairs to her hangout and tried to determine what she could do to get her mind off of David. He'd given her his business card. Maybe he had a website. She found the card in her purse and looked at it. 'House of David'. A clever name. A biblical implication that might attract people. He'd be a good marketing person.

When she typed in House of David.com a website popped up that looked rather amateurish but complete. All the necessary information and several photos of furniture. Impressive and beautiful pieces. For sure she'd have to visit the showroom. And maybe she could help him with a better website. That way she'd get to see him more often.

• • •

He fed the new table top into his surface planer, scattering wood shavings everywhere since he'd forgotten to turn on the shop vacuum. Oh well. He'd sweep it up later.

Maybe she'd show up at Starbucks on Friday. That was only two days away. Could he wait that long? Or maybe she'd need an Uber ride before then. He knew where she lived but dared not try to reach her. And he knew what building she worked in, but didn't even know the name of her business. Maybe if he entered her building, he could look at the occupant list and identify her company. But what good would that do?

He could pay a kid to slip a note under her office door. But where could he find a kid? And maybe there was a seal between the door and the floor. He'd just have to hope she'd be at Starbucks.

CHAPTER 18

Friday finally arrived, but not soon enough for David. He showered and paid extra attention when he was shaving. A new blade helped, along with the good-smelling Taylor's Sandalwood shaving cream, a splurge he didn't use very often. And Old Spice under his arms. He selected his fairly new blue work shirt that almost looked like a dress shirt, and his nicest work jeans.

When he got to the job site, his assignment was putting up 2X4 studs that divided the rooms. It was a one-person job, so he could take his break without disrupting anyone. He'd asked the day before if he could do this and his boss agreed.

After a ten-minute drive to Starbucks, he turned into a parking garage around the corner where there were plenty of empty stalls. A quick walk and he was approaching the building with the green and white logo on the door. It wasn't long before he was sitting at the counter sipping his whipped-cream-topped mocha, hoping she'd come.

• • •

Melanie kept watching the clock. It was 9:30. Fifteen minutes until zero hour, as she called it. She hadn't had time to do much at work, arriving just after 8:30, but she couldn't have accomplished much anyway.

Finally 9:45 appeared on the digital clock above her desk. Time to head out. She was old-fashioned and preferred clocks with hands on them, but having a digital one worked best at her job. She was soon out the door, locking it, and heading down the enclosed cement stairwell.

Moving onto the sidewalk, she found herself walking rather quickly but she didn't want to get there before 10. She concentrated on slowing down, and stopped to look in the window of the boutique. They'd changed the window display and she saw a nice-looking dark blue long-sleeve blouse that she'd check out later. She was too anxious to get to Starbucks.

When she arrived, David was sitting at the counter. What a relief!

She ordered her mocha, waited in line for it and headed for David.

"Excuse me sir. Is this seat taken?"

He was initially startled but quickly recovered. "Oh, no. Please take it. I'm just here by myself."

She climbed onto the stool and set her mocha on a napkin, resting her hands on the counter. David immediately went into his act of faking a cell phone call.

"I'm so glad you came. I missed you very much," he said, talking into his phone.

"I missed you too. Friday morning didn't come soon enough."

"Why don't you get your cell phone out and act like you're making a call."

She pulled it from her leather purse and held it to her ear.

"So what do we do now? Could we do another lunch at Bob's Lobster Shack?"

"I thought you'd never ask," she laughed. "That's exactly what was on my mind. That was so special for me the other day. Wednesday would be a good day for me."

"Okay. Same routine. I'll meet you at the drug store. But how will I get along until then?"

"I have a suggestion."

"You do?"

"Yes. I'd like to come and see what you're doing in your shop. Could I come by tomorrow, as a prospective customer?"

"That would make my day!"

"I'll call the number on your business card and inquire about stopping by. That way it will be an official business call. And we can also make arrangements for Wednesday at that time."

"You've already thought this out haven't you?"

"I have. We'll get to be together tomorrow and also next Wednesday."

"Great. I guess I have to get back to carpentering. But seeing you now will get me through the day. And hopefully the next few days. I can hardly wait."

"You're too funny. You sound like a little boy."

"Maybe sometimes I am. Especially around you."

He got up from his seat and headed for the glass door.

Melanie sat there for a few minutes while finishing her mocha, watching others use their computers, cell phones, or just chatting. She felt somewhat frightened about this adventure and where it was going. She pushed away from the counter, slid off the stool and headed for the door. Having been with David would help her get through the rest of the day.

. . .

That evening a call came to David's house that Ginny answered with 'House of David'.

"Hello, I was told about your wonderful furniture designs and I heard you had a showroom. I was wondering if I could stop by and see what you have available?"

"That's up to my husband. Let me put you through to him. He's out in the shop now."

A connection was made and David picked up. "Hello. House of David. May I help you?"

"Yes, my name is Melanie Johnson and I heard about your furniture designs. I was wondering if I could stop by sometime and see what you have available?"

"That would be fine. I'm generally in the shop on weekends and for sure will be here tomorrow. If you'd like to come by, I'd be happy to show you what I have. What time do you think you might be able to come?"

"I'll be running some errands in the early afternoon. Would two o'clock work?

"I'll definitely be here. My address is 410 Hawthorne Street. Just come directly to the garage. You'll see it behind the house. There's a doorbell you can use when you get here."

"Thank you very much. I'll look forward to it." She hung up.

He was caught off guard when she called, but they'd both handled the call very professionally. If Ginny had been listening, there's no way she would suspect anything.

He decided he'd better clean up the shop. Vacuuming, dusting, and sweeping kept him busy for the rest of the evening.

. . .

Ginny carefully hung up after the call ended. It sounded legitimate and she felt guilty listening. What was she looking for? A secret romance? She decided she wasn't doing anything exciting to keep David interested. Maybe some outside work would help instead of staying home with the kids. But what could she do? She had no experience or training in anything except mothering. And she had a busy life with all her committees and clubs. Pretty boring for David, she concluded.

CHAPTER 19

David was up bright and early, cooking French toast for the family on his cast iron griddle. The kids loved it, especially when he served it with bacon from his grill.

After they finished eating and the kids left, he sat at the table with Ginny, finishing his coffee.

"The woman that phoned last night. Is she coming by?"

"Yes, she said she would. Thanks for transferring the call. She said she'd be here around two o'clock. Hopefully she'll buy something. If so, we could go out to dinner. I wish we could afford a separate phone and answering machine for my shop so you wouldn't have to be bothered with calls."

"I don't mind. Especially when they lead to extra income. Unfortunately those calls don't come very often."

"I know. So what's on your agenda for the day?"

"Just the usual. Shopping and then my exercise class in the afternoon."

"I guess I'll head for the shop."

He left the table and headed out the back door. While walking to the garage he always stopped to check his garden. With the short growing season, he had to be selective about what he planted.

The lettuce and carrot seeds went in the ground in early May and his tomatoes and cucumbers were doing well. The climbing rose along the trellis was getting ready to bloom and his other roses were in full bloom. Overall, the garden looked pretty good.

He got his keys out and opened the shop door. The temperature inside was cool so he lit a fire in the wood stove, using a few logs to warm the place up. The stove was well sealed and vented so he didn't have to worry about smoke or other contaminants affecting his furniture.

The coffee table was almost finished and he was very satisfied with it. Next was spraying it, but he didn't want to have the lacquer fumes when Melanie came so he would do that later.

When lunch time rolled around he went to the house and had a beer and a sandwich. While eating he glanced at the clock above the sink realizing that she'd be there in just a little over an hour. This would be a new experience, having a woman at his house that he was attracted to other than his wife.

Back in the shop, the clock seemed to move slowly. He sharpened a few tools and checked the tension on the band saw.

Finally the doorbell rang.

. . .

Melanie did her usual Saturday morning routine. After fixing oatmeal for breakfast and cleaning up the dishes, she picked up a few of the kid's things and cleaned up around the house. Paul was off to his usual golf game so she was left with the kids. She'd decided they were old enough that she could leave them for short periods of time, leaving a cell phone that she'd taught Nellie how to use in an emergency. They'd experimented with it a few times and it worked well.

Whole Foods was her destination around 11 a.m. to purchase rib steaks to please Paul, along with baked potatoes and sour cream. Was she having the nice dinner to try to assuage her guilt?

When she returned from shopping, she fixed turkey sandwiches for the kids. They'd complain about not getting peanut butter and jelly but she wanted them to have at least one healthy lunch a week.

She kept looking at the clock, trying to encourage the hands to move faster but they wouldn't. At quarter past one she headed up to the bedroom to change. She didn't want to look too dressed up but also not too casual so she put on dressy jeans and a nice silk blouse and wore her hair in a ponytail held with a nice clip. And she'd also use very little makeup.

Google Maps said it was a 15-minute drive to David's shop. Her GPS would take her the best way.

At approximately 2 p.m. she arrived at his house and could see the garage at the end of a long gravel driveway. That must be The House of David.

Driving past the house, she noticed a very neat garden. It was David's responsibility if she remembered correctly, and it was very organized and neat. Not a weed in sight. The roses were beginning to bloom and she could see that he'd just planted tomatoes. What a green thumb he has.

After walking carefully on the gravel in her low heels, she stepped onto a large cement porch and pushed the doorbell button. It wasn't long before it opened and there he was.

"Hi. I'm Mrs. Johnson. I called about seeing your furniture."

"Yes. Please come in."

"You must be David? I can see that you have quite a nice shop."

"That's right," he said "Most of my tools are fairly old but they work well with proper care."

"They must be getting that, based on what I hear about the quality of your furniture."

"I assume that's a compliment and I'll take it. But you came to see what's in the showroom."

"Among other things, yes." She looked at him with a slight smile.

"It's over on this side. I have it separated with shower curtains so as not to get sawdust on the finished furniture." He took her hand and led her through the curtains. There were no windows in this area and after the curtains swung closed, he put his right arm around her waist and pulled her towards him, giving her a hug that she returned.

"I was hoping you'd do that."

"Me too. I wasn't sure how you'd react."

"Now you know."

"I'd like to show you what I have. A few small tables and chairs are mostly what I do at this point. Larger projects, such as buffets, table and chair sets, and chest of drawers are on the drawing board but they take time to build. Therefore a long delay before the money comes in."

"It's certainly beautiful furniture. I'm thinking about buying that chair over there but I'll have to speak with my husband about it. That would give me a reason to return," she whispered.

"I like that idea. And I'm looking forward to Wednesday."

"Me too."

"So how much are you asking for the chair?"

"$300."

"Is that all? I don't think you know what they're worth on the open market. You underestimate the quality of your work. I'll give you no less than $600. And no arguments."

"I don't know what to say. But if it's either that or no sale, I guess I'll have to take $600. From what you say, I should reconsider upping the price of all my pieces."

"You definitely should."

They headed back though the curtains and were standing next to each other when the door burst open.

"Dad! Dad! The Red Sox are whipping the Yankees...oops! I didn't know someone was here. I'm sorry to interrupt."

"That's OK, Gary. This is Mrs. Johnson. She's here to look at my furniture."

That was close. He'd almost given her another hug.

"Glad to hear the Red Sox are ahead. I'll root for them too."

"Thank you Ma'am. They can use all the help they can get. I'll head back to the game." He moved towards the door and then quickly turned around. "Nice to meet you"

"It's nice meeting you too, Gary. Bye now."

He was out the door, shutting it quietly.

"What a nice polite boy you have."

"Yes, he's very thoughtful."

"Like someone else I know. I guess I'd better get home. This will keep me going for the rest of the day. But what will I do tomorrow?"

"The same thing I'll be doing. Remembering today but also thinking about Wednesday."

"Yes. So I'll say goodbye."

When she approached the door, he pulled her towards him and gave her another hug, enjoying the feeling and not thinking about the consequences.

"That will keep me going. See you soon." She headed out the door.

"What's happening," he said to himself after she left. "We can't go on this way or we'll be basket cases."

CHAPTER 20

Sunday was a day David usually worked in the shop but today he wasn't in the mood. He needed to get away to take his mind off of Melanie.

He decided to propose that the family drive to the beach. The temperature was in the high seventies, unusual for this time of year, and there was very little wind.

At the breakfast table he brought up the subject. "It looks like a nice day. How about we go to the beach?"

"Yes!" Gary screamed.

"Great!" said Abby

"I'm certainly for it," said Ginny. "We haven't been yet this year. "I'll see what we have for a lunch. Where should we go?"

"Old Orchard Beach is always nice."

Both of the kids chimed in, "Yeah!"

"I'll get the blanket and beach umbrella together, as well as two beach chairs for us old folks."

"To get a good spot, we should head out as soon as we can."

"I can be ready in about 15 minutes," David said.

"It won't take me much longer than that."

Soon they were in the Murphy Hill area, heading east. The grassy, low-rolling hills allowed a nice view of Casco Bay. They passed a small gift shop with a large ice ream cone sign above the door. Near that was a beach store with kayaks and surfboards stacked in front. The Maine Narrow Gauge Railroad tourist train came into view. Old-fashioned brown Pullman cars pulled by a black steam engine.

"I wish we could take a ride on the train," said Gary.

"Not today. Wouldn't you rather spend time at the beach?"

"I guess so."

Abby piped up, "When we get there can we go to Playland?"

"Yes, but we don't have a lot of money so you'll have to be choosey about the rides."

"Maybe you could sell another table or a chair," said Gary. "Did that lady buy anything?"

"Yes, I was wondering about that," Ginny said. "I hope she did."

"She found a chair she liked but had to discuss it with her husband. It's probably a sale, but we can't spend the money until we have it."

"Let's just hope. While we're there, do you think you and I can walk out to the Patio Pub on the end of the pier and have a beer or a glass of wine and some snacks?"

"I think that could be arranged," David said.

When they arrived, parking spots were mostly taken on First Street but they saw one and grabbed it.

Gathering some things from the car, they headed for the beach, finding a spot about 20 yards from the ocean.

"I'll set up the umbrella while you spread the blankets. Then I'll go back to the car and get the beach chairs."

"A good plan," Ginny said. "And maybe Gary could carry the ice chest. It's not very heavy. Just four drinks and sandwiches. And Abby could bring that bag with the chips, plates, and dessert cookies."

"That would be great."

After they were settled, they watched the kids kicking up the sand with their toes as they moved quickly to the water, ignoring how cold it was.

"Let's take a walk along Old Orchard Street sometime during the afternoon."

"That sounds good to me," he said as he sat down in his beach chair and opened the latest thriller by Silfvast.

■ ■ ■

"Since you insisted that I not play golf today, what can we do instead of sitting around?"

Paul had a golf date later in the morning, but felt somewhat pressured to spend time with the family. His group was a foursome and they'd just have to play with three or possibly get a substitute.

"How about going to the beach?" Nellie said. She was thinking about seeing some cute boys.

"Sounds like a good idea," said Melanie. Anything to divert her attention from thinking about David.

"Yeah! A great suggestion."

"So what beach should we go to?"

"I like Old Orchard," said Nellie.

"That's a good one. Do you all agree?"

They chimed in with a yes.

Old Orchard Beach was always a favorite for them as a family, about a half hour drive from their house. Everyone changed into beach clothes, and gathered their beach paraphernalia. Paul got the blankets, the beach chairs, and an umbrella, and Melanie packed a lunch.

Melanie knew this would be a good thing, helping get her mind off of yesterday's experience.

When they got to Old Orchard, they luckily found a parking spot on First Street. It would be easy to transfer their gear to the beach.

After setting up blankets, beach chairs and an umbrella, Paul and Melanie settled into reading and watching the kids splashing in the cold ocean water.

■ ■ ■

Gary came running up to David and said, "Hey Dad, that lady who came by to look at your furniture yesterday is down the beach from us. Maybe you could find out if she's going to buy the chair."

David was startled but tried not to show it.

"Why don't you go ask her, or should I tell her you're here, and maybe she'd come by and let you know?"

"What a coincidence but I don't think I should interrupt her day. She said she'd get back to me when she made a decision."

"But think, Dad. If we knew she wanted the chair we could have enough money to have more fun while we're here."

"I think Gary has a good point. Maybe she's made her decision. She wouldn't mind if you asked her. If you go, tell her to stop by with her family. Being friendly might help the sale."

He wondered what to do? If Melanie didn't see Gary she wouldn't know they were nearby. But if she did, or if Gary went near them again, she might recognize him and she'd wonder why I didn't stop by.

He decided he'd better approach her. Gary would be with him so that would make it easier. He got up and asked Gary to lead the way.

He saw her sitting with her husband, looking quite comfortable and as stunning as ever. He wondered if she came to the beach for the same reason he did.

As they approached, she turned towards them, did a slight, imperceptible jerk of her head, and smiled.

David approached and said, "Hello Mrs. Johnson. What a coincidence meeting you here. What a great day to visit the beach. My son noticed you when he passed by."

"Yes, it's quite a surprise to see you." More proof that we like the same things, she thought. "This is my husband, Paul. This is Mr. Stevens, David Stevens I think it is. The man that makes the nice furniture, and this is his son. Is it Gary?

Gary broke into a smile. She remembered his name. He politely said, "Yes. It's nice to see you again."

"Honey, I stopped by yesterday and looked at the furniture he had for sale in his showroom. I haven't had a chance to discuss it with you yet but I found a chair that I like very much."

"I'm not surprised. Of course you'll probably buy whatever you like. I always appreciate the things you choose though, so I'll leave that up to you. How much is the chair?"

"It's $600. Not inexpensive, but the price is not out of line with other furniture of that quality."

"$600 for a chair? Well, as I said, I'll leave that up to you."

She turned to David and said, "I'll let you know soon. I'm trying to decide if I have a place to put it."

"I'm certainly not rushing you. It was my son who convinced me that we should stop by."

"I'm glad you did." He noticed a faint smile.

He felt obligated to say something more. "If you'd like to meet the rest of my family, come on up the beach and I'll introduce you. I guess Gary and I will head back to our spot."

"Nice meeting you Mr. Stevens, or should I call you David,"

"Anything works for me."

After they left, Paul turned to Melanie and said, "Is that his main business or what does he do for a living?"

"He's a carpenter. But apparently his furniture business isn't sufficiently profitable for him to be a furniture craftsman full time so he builds houses. He also drives Uber part time. That's how I met him. He picked me up at the airport on one of my business trips. That's when he gave me his furniture business card. I guess it's a good way for him to get the word out."

Melanie was anxious to meet David's wife so she and Paul headed up the beach. She could see David sitting under an umbrella next to a fairly attractive woman so she motioned Paul to follow her.

"Hi again Mr. Stevens, I brought my husband along to meet your wife." She approached and walked up to Ginny. Ginny immediately got up and brushed herself off. She was wearing an attractive blue bathing suit and had her dark hair pulled back in a pony tail.

"Hi, I'm Melanie Johnson and this is my husband, Paul. I called the other night to inquire about your husband's furniture and you transferred me to his shop phone. I stopped by his showroom yesterday to look at his furniture."

"Yes, I remember. I hope you found something you liked."

"He had a chair that I really liked and I've almost decided to buy it, as I told your husband and son a few minutes ago."

"That's great. It's nice meeting you." She didn't offer her hand and began sitting back down in her beach chair, implying the conversation was over. She didn't like the idea of an attractive woman coming to their garage, as she sometimes referred to it. David also came in contact with attractive women on his Uber runs, but meeting women at his shop bothered her more.

"It was nice meeting you," Melanie said, as she and Paul turned and headed back down the beach.

"A rather defensive woman," she said to Paul.

"Yes, that was fairly obvious. Maybe seeing an attractive woman like you visiting her husband in his garage made her nervous. I guess I would feel the same way if an attractive guy, such as Stevens, visited with you in our garage." He laughed but also thought seriously about what he had just said. The guy was for sure no slouch. In fact he looked a little like Robert Redford.

They arrived back at their blanket and sat down.

CHAPTER 21

Melanie arrived at her office on Monday morning at 8:30. Sitting at her desk, she began to plan the day. After some thought, she added one item to her agenda: go to Starbucks around 10. David wouldn't be there but if she were seen there on a regular basis, it wouldn't be as noticeable when she sat next to him on Fridays. The extra exercise would be good for her.

Meeting him and his family at the beach was shocking. She encouraged her family to go to the beach to get her mind of off him, and he ends up a few yards away. Why did he choose that beach? And why was his family only a short distance away from hers? Since it's such an extensive beach, either of them could have been a quarter of a mile either up or down the beach and they would have never run into each other. And if Gary hadn't barged in on them in David's shop on Saturday, he wouldn't have noticed her at the beach. Too much to deal with.

It was 9:45. Time to head down the street.

She put on a light sweater, locked her door as she left, and headed for the stairwell. It wasn't very wide, with hand rails on both sides. She paid attention because she'd fallen on stairs when the was a child and her mother taught her to always use the hand rail.

Arriving at the lobby, she noticed the elevator, several rows of mailboxes, and the door to the outside. No doorman like New York City she thought. Too fancy for Portland.

Walking along Congress Street she could see Monument Square and Starbucks ahead. She entered and headed directly to the ordering line. When her turn came, the server said, "A Grande low-fat mocha?"

"How did you remember?"

"That's what we do here. We aim to please."

"I guess you should also give me a slice of that fluffy-looking coffee cake on the top shelf."

"Coming right up. You know where to pick up your mocha. And here's your coffee cake." She handed it to her in a slim paper bag.

Melanie paid and moved to the pickup line. When her drink was ready, she headed for their usual counter away from the window.

After finishing her snack it was back to the office, strolling slowly up Congress Street, thinking about the Wednesday lunch.

■ ■ ■

David couldn't get his mind off of meeting Melanie at the beach. Was it a coincidence or was it meant to be? He couldn't decide whether it was a good or bad thing to happen. Ginny got to meet Melanie and he wasn't sure what she thought.

He'd have to be careful about how he dealt with that.

While driving to his job he was thinking about lunch on Wednesday. He knew he'd have trouble concentrating until then. When arriving at the site, he strapped his leather tool belt around his waist and headed into the building. It was a two-story colonial-style house with an attached three-car garage. What would they possibly do with five bedrooms and three cars? He knew the owners only had two kids. That leaves two extra bedrooms. One of them couldn't be an office since they had a place for an office on the main floor. Maybe it was the image they wanted to project to the community.

Seeing Melanie sitting on the beach was disturbing, to say

the least. The two-piece blue bathing suit she wore wasn't overly skimpy but showed enough to cause some unease. What an attractive figure. Lucky Paul, if that was his name. David hadn't paid much attention to him. How could someone be interested mainly in sports with that attractive woman around?

As he'd approached them sitting in their wooden-armed beach chairs on Sunday, she'd quickly put a towel over her thighs. She was so modest. Did she really know how attractive she was?

Time to get to work. He set up two saw horses, moved several two by fours onto them, measured, and began to cut a number of studs for the maid's quarters. Losing his concentration, he accidentally cut one of them too short. He'd have to pay more attention.

Hurry up and come, Wednesday!

CHAPTER 22

When he awakened, his first thought was: It's finally Wednesday! He jumped out of bed and dashed into the bathroom. Why was he moving so fast? He wouldn't see her until noon. Pulling off his shorts, he stepped into the tiled shower, enjoying the warm water cascading over his head. He loved the smell of his pine-scented soap.

Slipping into his nicest work jeans and a clean shirt, he headed downstairs. He didn't want to look too dressed up for fear Ginny would be suspicious. He had his usual breakfast and was soon out the door, wearing a hat but no jacket. He took a sip of coffee from his tall stainless-steel coffee mug before slipping it into the cup holder. He decided it tasted extra good. Maybe that had something to do with the agenda for the day.

• • •

Melanie awoke, looked around and saw that Paul was already up. He'd finished in the bathroom, so she swung herself onto the edge of the bed, her feet almost reaching the floor, and rubbed her eyes.

She remembered it was Wednesday. Quickly sliding to the floor, she pulled the bed spread over the pillows and headed for the bathroom. What would she wear? She thought about it while brushing her teeth and decided on cream-colored jeans and a yellow blouse. She knew she'd be doing some walking so she chose comfortable brown sandals. Brushing her hair into a pony tail, she tied it with a bright yellow ribbon. She alternated between a pony tail and a bun when going to her office, depending upon her mood.

Yogurt, a half piece of toast with apricot jam, and a glass of juice satisfied her. She'd have her coffee later.

The kids arrived in the kitchen as she was getting out the cereal bowls and juice glasses.

"What kind of cereal today? Raisin Bran or Cheerios?"

"Oh, Mom. Why can't we have what our friends have? Frosted Flakes or something like that?"

"Because they have too much sugar. You know that's not good for you. And you'll probably make it up later with a candy bar or ice cream."

They reluctantly dished up the cereal, drank the juice and grabbed their lunch money and back-packs.

"Give me a kiss."

They both kissed her on the cheek and were off.

Melanie had the house to herself. It was very quiet as she sat there contemplating her day as she sipped her coffee.

"I know I shouldn't be doing this but I can't seem to help it. He fascinates me. It's not just a sexual attraction. He's so unassuming and seems to be very confident, except with his woodworking business. It apparently is more of a hobby since he can't make a living at it. He has no idea of how good he is. Maybe I'll be able to get over these feelings after lunch. I'll try to say something to end it. But what?"

She left the house carrying her portfolio and her purse. With luck she'd find a parking spot behind her building.

The rear entrance to her building was locked, so she walked slowly around to the front. While doing that, she decided to let the situation evolve as things happened and not try to generate too many pros and cons beforehand. That thought relaxed her by the time she got to the stairs.

In her office she had trouble concentrating, continually watching the clock. At 11:30 she folded up her work, cleared off her desk and prepared to leave.

As she headed for the corner of Congress and High Street she decided she could still back out by not getting on the bus.

Arriving at the Square, it was always such a pleasant place with the monuments and various temporary displays. It gave her a good feeling, and today she definitely needed good feelings since she was so undecided about what to do.

When the blue bus pulled up, she hesitated and then climbed on. She again headed to a vacant rear seat since she didn't want to speak with anyone.

The first part of the route was mainly commercial buildings but then they came to a residential area. Nice houses with neat lawns. Seeing the Westgate Plaza approaching, she prepared to get off. After a short walk to the pharmacy, she felt comfortable entering the store and heading for the cosmetic section.

CHAPTER 23

When David entered the drug store, he saw Melanie wandering through the cosmetics aisles. He slowly approached her. After briefly holding her hand, they walked out together.

"I didn't want to say much and I guess we shouldn't have held hands but I couldn't help it. I was so happy to see you."

"I felt the same way. I'm excited about our lunch date."

"So it's okay to call it a date now?"

"I guess I'm being realistic, because that's what it is. Think of it any way you want but it's a date."

"Fine with me."

By the time they got to his car they were holding hands again but not saying much, although many thoughts were going through their heads. He opened the passenger door, watched her slide in, slowly closed it and moved around to his side. As he slid in, he caught site of her beautiful smile.

"It's so good to see you, to be with you. This is practically all I've been thinking about since Sunday."

"Me too." After a brief moment, he started the car. They didn't say much during the 20-minute ride. They were just enjoying being together.

When he pulled into the restaurant parking lot, he jumped out and came around to do his usual door opening.

"Thank you Sir."

"My pleasure."

They chose a table overlooking the water. A romantic setting.

The server soon appeared. "Can I get you something to drink before taking your orders?"

"Do we both want wine? I enjoyed it last time, even though I'm not used to it," David said.

"Yes, why don't you bring us both a glass of your house Chardonnay," Melanie responded.

The server looked at them and smiled. Their attraction to each other was obvious. So were the wedding rings they were both wearing. They could be newlyweds but she didn't think so.

"What are you thinking about having?" she asked as she reached for his hand.

"You," he quickly said. "No. Sorry, I couldn't help it. It just came out."

"That was cute," she replied, smiling. "I think it's lobster time for me. I'll have a small one and a cup of the clam chowder."

"I'll have the sea bass and also the chowder."

When the server returned with the wine, they gave her their orders.

After a few minutes of silence, just staring at each other and looking at the scenic ocean views, Melanie said, "We don't seem to need to talk. Just being together is enough."

"You're right. I wish we could make it happen more often."

"So do I."

"I've been thinking about something but reluctant to bring it up."

"Oh. This sounds serious."

"You won't walk out on me for mentioning it?"

"It depends on what it is. If it's to commit a crime, I think I'll pass. What is it?"

"I have a cabin that I built at Moosehead Lake about ten years ago. Our family used it regularly but now that the kids are older they don't want to go and Ginny isn't thrilled about going either.

She tells me I should go by myself and get it out of my system. Chopping wood, fishing, frying the fish I catch and whatever."

"It sounds like an exciting place. But what does that have to do with me? Oh. Do I know where you're going with this?"

"It sounds like you do. If I go, it would be for a long weekend so I wouldn't miss much work. I have to go sometime soon to open it up and check it out. Would you consider going with me? I'm not talking about a romantic adventure. The cabin has two bedrooms. We'd just take walks, fix meals and enjoy being together. Sitting out at night. Those are my thoughts."

"Wow. That's quite an offer. It would certainly be advancing our relationship a few notches."

"I didn't quite know how to bring it up but you provided the opening. So it's your fault."

"You can't blame me, but I can understand why you were uncomfortable raising the possibility."

"Very uncomfortable."

"I certainly can't give you an answer now but it does sound intriguing. I'll think about it and let you know. Maybe when we're at Starbucks. But one thing comes to mind. If we were to do this, when would it happen?"

"I was thinking as soon as the next weekend, not the coming one but the one after that."

"I'd have to use the excuse of attending a two-day seminar in New York. Those often happen and I usually don't go. But I've mentioned them to Paul before so it wouldn't be something new."

"Great idea."

"Here you go again, getting me thinking about the details rather than the trip itself. For me it would be a significant event.

"Certainly, for me too."

The server brought their food and they began quietly eating.

After a short time, Melanie began laughing. "I think we're both so overwhelmed by your proposal that we don't know what to say. So why don't we change the subject. Do you wonder why we ended up so near each other at the beach on Sunday? I think it wasn't just chance. It was meant to be."

"Too many things had to happen for our families to end up that close to each other."

"So how do you feel about it? Are you glad it happened?"

"I'm happy that Ginny got to meet you and vice versa. It makes things a little easier for me."

"And I'm glad Paul got to meet my furniture designer. If our spouses only knew what's going on between us. I certainly hope they don't."

"Me too."

"Are we going to meet somewhere else in addition to the beach, or possibly Moosehead Lake? Accidentally that is? Do you ever think some things are preordained?"

"I don't know, but if that's the reason I met you, I'm glad it happened."

She patted her mouth with the napkin. "The lobster is very good, but a little messy. I should have ordered it shelled. What about your sea bass?

"It's excellent. I haven't had it for a while since we don't get to eat expensive fish very often, but I'm not complaining. It's just a fact of life for us."

After they finished their meals, the server removed their plates and asked if they wanted dessert. They both declined.

"Holding hands briefly with you is my dessert," David said.

"That's what I was looking forward to all morning."

After paying their checks, David put his arm around her waist as they headed outside, appreciating the opportunity to touch her.

She turned to him and smiled. "I like that."

On their way back to the city, Melanie said, "I can't get the thought of Moosehead Lake out of my mind. You shouldn't have sprung that on me. It sounds too good to be true."

"I thought about mentioning it but I was too chicken. Then

it just came out."

"I can understand your reluctance, but I'm so glad you did. We'll just have to see what happens."

"I hope you can work it out. I'd love for you to see my little cabin. It has a small kitchen, a living area with a rustic stone fireplace, two bedrooms and a bath with a shower. And an outside shower. You'd have to share a bathroom with me, not at the same time, of course."

She chuckled. She was amused when he stumbled over words relating to their relationship.

He pulled up to the pharmacy and parked in the rear to minimize being seen. He opened her door and when she got out, he pulled her to him in a big hug. He wanted to kiss her but thought that wouldn't be appropriate.

"Bye for now," she whispered. "Will I see you at Starbucks on Friday?"

"I wouldn't miss it for anything." He got into his car and drove off.

Melanie walked to the bus stop and noticed on the posted schedule that a bus would arrive in about five minutes. When the big blue bus pulled up, she again went to the rear. Choosing a window seat, she began thinking about what had just happened. It was a wonderful time. But staying with him for a weekend? That might be pushing things.

Arriving at her office, she hardly felt like working. She had to force herself. Looking at their calendar for the next weekend, Paul had a golf tournament on Sunday that would keep him busy.

What am I doing? Already planning to be away with David?

CHAPTER 24

David had always looked forward to Saturdays in his shop. Now, his anticipation changed to Fridays. He put on a tan long-sleeved work shirt, and his best jeans. In the bathroom he did an extra trim on his beard, and combed his hair loosely to the side, the casual look.

After finishing breakfast, he took his full coffee mug and headed for his car. It was two hours before he'd see that awesome smile and those deep brown eyes. Even before meeting Melanie, he'd always looked forward to his visits to Starbucks. The customers were either involved in serious conversations, stuffing coffee cake into their mouths, or concentrating on either their laptop or their cell phone, as opposed to his usual activity of pounding nails.

He pulled up to the job site, parking in ruts of mud near the curb. Someone must have had watered down the area to control the dust. Stepping carefully when he got out, he was thinking his work might go slowly until ten.

▪ ▪ ▪

When Melanie awakened, a smile spread across her face. She realized that Friday had finally arrived and she'd be meeting that attractive guy with the soft-spoken voice and the wispy hair. Would she try to sit on the wooden stool next to him, or should she sit farther away?

Jumping out of bed and slipping out of her pink pajama top, she headed for the bathroom. She was usually modest and didn't go parading around the bedroom naked, especially with Paul around, but he was already downstairs.

After dressing and fixing her hair, she went quickly down the carpeted stairs, sliding her hand along the polished wooden banister. She was stepping rather lightly while humming a tune. Paul had probably left for work so he wouldn't be around to notice her demeanor.

She grabbed a strawberry yogurt from the fridge and poured orange juice to have with her vitamins. Next came a cup of Dunkin' Donuts dark roast coffee, her favorite blend.

The kids crunched down on their cereal, gulped down their juice, grabbed their backpacks, and headed for the door.

"Bye, Mom," Nellie yelled.

"Have a nice day," Melanie replied.

Josh came up and gave her a peck on the cheek and said, "Bye Mom, I love you." He was so sensitive. Probably takes after me, she thought.

"I love you too, very much."

Time to head to the office. She grabbed her leather bag and large brown leather portfolio and moved to the back door, stopping to peer out the window at the attractive green grass and flowers in the backyard. Paul took good care of the lawn and she did the roses.

Before stepping outside, she slung a light-colored sweater over her shoulder. Once out, the smell of the fresh cut grass engulfed her. Paul had just mowed the lawn the day before.

She backed out of the graveled driveway. Paul always intended to make a turnaround but she didn't mind backing up.

She loved driving her Subaru with all-wheel drive, which she sometimes needed in the snowy and icy Maine winters. The car had a sun-roof that she used in the summer. Just push a button and she almost had a convertible. But the feature she liked most was a back-up camera, and the car still had the new smell.

She saw a parking place next to her building. Someone must have just pulled out.

She was soon looking at her office door: Melanie Johnson, Graphic Designs and Commercial Advertising. As if anyone would ever read it, or even need to read it, she thought, since her business was in New York and other big cities. Probably no one in Portland could afford her.

Her small office was very simple. White walls with a window behind a comfortable wooden desk and next to that her drafting table. A few scenic pictures hung on the walls and only room for two additional chairs.

After she sat down she placed her hands on the polished wooden desktop, interlaced her fingers, and began thinking about Starbucks and David. She knew the subject of spending the next weekend at his cabin would come up. What should she do? A weekend at a remote location in the woods sounded tantalizing, especially with David.

CHAPTER 25

He glanced at his watch while installing a large wooden header above one of the window openings. It was 9:15. Normally the time of day didn't matter, but not today. In 45-minutes he would get to see her beautiful smile.

At 9:30, he put his hammer, Skil-Saw and tool belt in the wooden tool bin and eagerly drove to Congress Street. He hoped he'd find a parking space, but if not, the parking garage would work.

When arriving at Monument Square, with its attractive statues and brick walkways, he began looking for parking. As he turned the corner onto Free Street, a red Toyota pulled out, not far from Starbucks. Today's my lucky day, he thought.

He parallel parked, locked the car and approached the stone building on the corner. He'd read once that the worst thing about parallel parking was the witnesses. That made him laugh.

Upon entering Starbucks, he moved to the ordering line. His turn quickly came, and a person in a green-apron said, "Are you having your usual, a Venti mocha?"

"You got it. And I'll have a chocolate croissant to go with it."

"That'll be seven dollars. I'll get your croissant and you know where to pick up your drink."

"Thanks for the quick service."

"I guess you haven't been here when the lunch crowd arrives. You wouldn't be saying that."

He moved to the pickup line. When his drink came he chose to sit at

an interior counter not facing the window. No one else was sitting there.

Slowly sipping his drink, he found himself staring at the green

Starbucks design, a well-known marketing symbol.

He heard a familiar voice. "You're all alone. Could you use some company?" she whispered.

"If it's a beautiful woman with dusty blond hair, the answer is definitely yes!"

"Perhaps I'll sit one seat away, at the end of the counter. A more handsome man might come by."

"Good idea." He noticed the attractive jade bracelet and necklace she was wearing. It went well with the cream-colored blouse. He couldn't help looking at the blouse.

David got his cell phone out and pretended to be making a call while Melanie feigned texting someone.

"So how has your day been going so far? Any cuts or bruises?"

"No, I managed to saw a few straight boards, and pound some nails without smashing my thumb."

"Is that what happens on a normal day?"

"No, just when I'm thinking about you. But that's beginning to be a normal day lately."

"I can certainly relate to that." She took a sip of her mocha and a bite of fresh pumpkin bread. "Apparently they always have this pumpkin bread. Have you tried it? It's very good."

"Are you a marketing agent for Starbucks?"

"No but I wish I had their account. That would be a big one so I'd need a few other people to help me."

They were both avoiding the subject they knew had to be addressed.

A woman approached and slid into the seat between them. She had short brown, slightly curly hair and a tan complexion, perhaps from being in the sun. And not unattractive.

"Hi Melanie, what are you doing here? I don't remember seeing you here before."

"Oh, hi Joanne. I've been coming once in a while lately, partially for the exercise, since my office is five blocks away, and partially for their good mochas."

"Too bad you're not sitting where I am, next to this good-looking man."

David overheard her and turned. "Why that's the nicest compliment I've had in the last hour."

The three of them laughed.

"I don't usually speak to strangers, but I think I could make an exception in this case," David said.

Joanne was flattered. She smiled and said, "I hope so. My name is Joanne, and yours?"

"I'm David, and the lovely lady next to you?"

"Oh, I'm Melanie. Just enjoying my mocha. Joanne and I are neighbors."

"So, you must work around here?" he said to Joanne.

"I do. At the People's United Bank on Congress Street."

"That's right across from my office," Melanie said.

"What a coincidence. Maybe we could have coffee together once in a while."

"I'd like that. I especially like to take a break around ten," Melanie said.

"A coincidence. That's when I come here on Fridays," said David. "Maybe I'll see both of you again sometime." Especially the one on the other side of Joanne, he thought.

"I've got to be going. I only get a short break since I'm just a teller." She got off of her stool and gave both of them a look. "I think you'd better watch out for this guy," she said as she looked at Melanie. "He could be dangerous."

"I'll certainly do that," Melanie replied. "Bye for now. It was nice seeing you."

"Yes, a pleasant surprise." She turned to David. "And maybe I should try to come here on Fridays more often. But my usual break isn't until 10:30 so that probably wouldn't work. Nice meeting you David. And by the way, I didn't get what you do?"

"Oh, nothing very exciting. I'm just a carpenter."

"You mean you build houses? Rather unusual to see someone like you here."

"Really?"

"Oh, I didn't mean it that way. I just thought that the people here at Starbucks all worked nearby."

"That's okay. I guess I'm different. I just pound nails, so to speak."

"Well, whoever get's one of your houses certainly must get a well-built one."

"I try. That's all I can say."

Melanie almost said: He mainly designs and builds creative furniture. She barely caught herself.

Joanne said goodbye and left.

"That was a close call. I didn't know she worked around here. It's good we were sitting apart."

"You're right. She seems like a nice person, but a little nosy."

"She lives a few houses up the street from me. She's a friendly neighbor, not someone I see often."

They sat without speaking for a short time. "That made me a little nervous. We've got to be careful," Melanie said.

"I don't think that'll be a problem at Moosehead Lake."

"There you go again, assuming I've agreed to the trip."

"But we'll have to do it so we can see each other, since we can't keep meeting here all the time, with the possibility of Joanne getting in our way."

"Okay. I'll bite the bullet. I'd like to go with you next weekend, provided it's as friends. You said the cabin has separate bedrooms and I can agree as long as that's the situation. But being with you and staying in the woods sounds very exciting."

"Am I hearing you correctly? I don't know what to say, other than I guess I'm surprised and very happy. We're both risking a lot to do this, but apparently you feel as compelled as I do."

"Not many people have the opportunity to spend time at a small cabin in the woods."

"I should mention that the Moosehead Lake area is very remote. There's only one grocery store that I know of, and that's on the south end of the lake. My cabin is about halfway up the west side. The deep blue lake is quite big. About 40 miles long by 3 miles wide. And it's secluded where we'd be."

"Good for us. I don't think I've ever been anywhere near that area. We've been to Rangeley Lake a few times but that's much closer to Portland."

"I could pick you up as your Uber driver, as though you were going to New York "

"Yes, and I'd have to take a small, carry-on suitcase to look business-like."

"I don't think you'll need much in the way of clothes. Oops. I didn't mean it that way. I meant maybe take only one change of clothes. We won't be going anywhere fancy."

"And I won't get much use of my dark gray suit, but it has to be my costume during departure and return."

"It will be safe at my cabin. And if you'd like to change in my car while we're driving, that would be fine with me."

"I'll bet it would. So a change of clothes, pajamas and a robe, both a light and a warm jacket, a hat, slippers, and toiletries. Does that sound like about it?"

"And good walking shoes. That all sounds good to me."

There was a pause in the conversation while all the ramifications settled in.

"I guess we won't be doing Starbucks here next Friday."

"No, but I'm one step ahead of you. I looked into it and there's one in Augusta, about an hour's drive from here. It's just off I-95 so it'll be easy to get to."

"You mean you've been planning this in advance?"

"Not until you said you'd think about it. That's when my life changed. A whole new world has opened up."

"You're being too dramatic. But I'll have to admit, mine has changed also. And there's one more thing before I have to get back to work. Could I possibly come by your shop either tomorrow or Sunday and purchase that beautiful maple chair?"

"I'd be delighted if you did."

"I thought maybe we'd have some last-minute things to discuss. And I definitely want the chair."

"It's a deal. Why don't you call first to make it official? Ginny will most likely answer the phone and direct your call to me and I'll be anxiously waiting."

"Great." She got up from her stool, said goodbye, and headed for the door.

After she was gone he turned around on his stool and watched as she passed by the front window. Was he a lucky man, or what?

CHAPTER 26

Friday evening Melanie had a pepperoni pizza and a green salad delivered. The kids loved the pepperoni but didn't particularly care for the salad so she'd add their favorite vegetables, olives, peppers, tomatoes, carrot slices, and chopped celery.

"Why do you always pick out the things you like in the salad and leave the rest. I could just as well give you a bowl of olives, celery and carrots. I should make you eat it all or not give you dessert."

"I hope that's a future threat but not tonight," said Josh.

"It's Friday night so you'll get dessert. It's vanilla ice cream with hot fudge sauce."

When the pizza came and the kids grabbed their pizza and began chowing down, whereas Paul and Melanie were polite but also anxious to have their first bite.

Melanie soon had four bowls of ice cream with fudge sauce on the table. The kids grabbed their servings and left. At that point, she and Paul were spooning the dessert into their mouths.

"There's a Red Sox game at 7:30 so I'll be heading into the family room."

"Before you go, I'd like to discuss the purchase of that chair. I'd like to buy it, but you didn't sound too happy about it the other day."

"I just thought $600 was a little high for a simple wood chair, but you have money and we're not hurting for cash, so go ahead and do it. Is it made by that guy we met at the beach, the Uber driver?"

"Yes, but that's not his regular profession. He designs and sells custom-made wood furniture." She chose not to remind him that David was a carpenter.

"If you were buying reserved seat tickets behind home plate at Fenway Park, that would be another matter. I'd certainly support that." He smiled, finished his ice cream, and headed for the family room.

• • •

David was thinking how wonderful it had been to see her at Starbucks. But how could he get through the next week until Friday? He hoped she might come by before then to purchase the chair.

He'd tell Ginny at dinner that he'd be going to the cabin next Friday, returning on Monday.

The four of them sat down at the dinner table with a large pizza. Not an uncommon meal for them on a Friday night.

"I hope you kids will eat this vegetable pizza. It's not what I usually order but I think you'll like it. If not, you'll just have to go hungry."

She opened the steaming box from Papa John's and placed it in the middle of the table, scooped up large slices for all of them. Paper plates worked well with pizza. Fewer dishes for a Friday night.

David had a beer, Ginny an iced tea, and the kids got to have cokes, a treat for them.

"The pizza's not bad," Gary said.

"Yeah," said Abby.

"It's sometimes nice to try new things," David said, wondering where his 'new thing' was taking him.

When they finished the pizza, Ginny got out graham cracker-crusted ice cream sandwiches from the freezer and passed them out. "Here's your reward for trying the veggie pizza."

"Thanks, Mom," Abby said. Gary also thanked her and they left for their rooms, most likely Gary to his computer games and Abby to her cell phone.

"I think I'll go to the cabin next weekend to open it up for the season. Would you like to go with me?"

"I don't think so. Gary has a baseball game and Abby has her dance lessons. You go ahead. I know it has to be opened up for the summer and you can get some fishing done."

"I thought I'd go Friday and return Monday. A few repairs will take some time." He wasn't lying. There were some things that needed fixing, but he probably wouldn't get to them.

It was still light enough that he went outside and tended the garden, mainly weeding. He loved working in his garden. It was very relaxing. He mostly planted vegetables from seed, including lettuce, carrots and peppers, and enjoyed watching them sprout and grow. He got the tomato plants from a nursery. The garden was located next to the stone patio where they had two chaise lounges. He used his quite often in the summer evenings, either reading or just looking at the sky.

Later, while reclining on his chaise, he was planning their escape, which occupied his mind for the rest of the evening.

"I want another beer," he said to himself. He got up from his chaise and went inside, grabbed a Negro Modelo, and headed back, popping the cap with his hand.

He preferred beer to wine or hard liquor but had to admit that having wine with Melanie was nice.

The stars were coming out when he returned to the chaise. He slumped onto the comfortable pad while staring up at the heavens. There was no moon but the stars were awesome, the same as Melanie.

CHAPTER 27

Sunday didn't come around soon enough for Melanie. She often went to church but not this day. It wouldn't have meant much. She knew she'd be thinking about David.

Paul was off to his golf game and the kids were hanging out with friends. She fussed around while finishing the breakfast dishes. Then swept the kitchen floor, a ceramic tile that cleaned up easily.

She liked her kitchen. Dark maple cabinets and medium colored, easy to clean granite countertops. An island located across from the sink had a butcher block cutting board that worked great for chopping vegetables. A large oak table was located just beyond the bar, surrounded by six spindle-backed chairs.

She wished she'd been able to hire David to make the cabinets. Did he do that kind of work? That could be too dangerous to have him working at their house.

She decided that working in the garden would kill time until early afternoon. She put on old jeans and a long-sleeved shirt. Her gardening shoes were in the garage.

After weeding she pruned the roses. The yellow begonias and white lilies were doing well and she hoped the pretty blue/purple lupine seeds would sprout soon.

She loved the white iron bench Paul had put in the far corner of the yard with the wooden arbor arching over it. The bright yellow rosebush covered it nicely and she sometimes sat there in the morning with a cup of coffee. That didn't happen often but she found it to be very relaxing.

When noon approached, the kids were off somewhere so she decided she could kill time by fixing herself a nice lunch, and by that she meant something that would take time to prepare.

She fixed a small lettuce, red pepper, and tomato salad to start with, and then a grilled cheese sandwich on sourdough bread. She'd take it to the garden to eat under the arbor.

There was no table to put her lunch on so she placed it on the bench next to her. After enjoying the salad, she started on the grilled cheese and began to ponder her situation.

"What's happening to me," she spoke softly to herself. "What were the chances of getting David as my Uber driver that day? He could have stayed at his carpentering job or he could have been driving around somewhere else looking for passengers."

She knew that when a person texted, the nearest Uber driver generally got the notification. So he had to be near the airport when she texted for a ride. And then, while heading to her house, that near accident brought them together. Was it fate? What else could it have been? He was such an interesting person. And a great furniture designer and builder. Pretty unusual.

At 1:30 she finally made the call to David's house.

"Hello, is this The House of David furniture shop?"

"Yes, you've reached the right place. Let me switch you out to the shop. I'm sure David will help you." Ginny pressed the button.

. . .

David's day was moving along slower than usual. Normally he got so engrossed in his woodworking that time went by quickly, and before long, it would be lunchtime. But not today. His mind was elsewhere. Mainly at the cabin and thinking about what it would be like for the two of them to be there.

He finished the long coffee table and placed it in his showroom. He was pleased how well the dark streaked wood patterns on the light-colored table-top showed up. A prize for the person who bought it. He decided he should start on a pair of end tables of the same wood. Maybe someone would want all three of them.

It was noon when he went into the house for lunch. The kids had eaten peanut butter and honey sandwiches and an apple, washing it down with a glass of milk. Ginny hadn't come back from church, so he was having lunch alone, a hot dog that he'd heated in the microwave. It was normally a favorite treat on the weekend, but today he didn't pay much attention to it even though he'd included a beer. He was looking forward to a particular call, waiting all morning but not expecting it until the afternoon, if at all.

Ginny walked in and dropped her purse on the chair. "I'm hungry."

"I just had a hot dog and a beer. I'd have waited if I'd known you were going to be here. I'm heading out to the shop."

When he got there he sat down at his desk and began working on a new buffet design. It would be a challenge but he'd had several inquiries about making such a piece so he decided to accept the challenge.

About 1:30 the phone rang. He grabbed it and said "House of David. May I help you?"

A familiar voice replied, "This is Mrs. Johnson. I visited your showroom over a week ago and fell in love with a particular chair you had."

"Oh, yes. I remember. You wanted the spindle-backed chair and offered to pay more than I was asking. And I saw you at the beach last Sunday."

"Yes. That's me."

He heard the transfer connection click off. Ginny apparently had been listening.

"I'm calling to see if you still have the chair. If so, I'd like to buy it."

"You're in luck." He'd put it away so no one else could purchase it until Melanie made up her mind.

"Could I pick it up today?"

"I'll be here all afternoon so you can come by any time. Just come to the shop and ring the bell. You know the routine. And you won't have to drive your car into the driveway since I'll gladly carry it to your car."

"Will you take a check?"

"As long as you tell me it won't bounce." He chuckled. "I'd be happy to take a check."

"Thank you. I'll be there later. Goodbye," and she hung up.

"She wants the chair. And more importantly, I'll get to see her."

He went back to his drawing board and found he was more productive. Just hearing her voice improved his mood considerably.

About 4:30 there was a knock on the door and he was there instantly, opening it to see her standing there with a wide smile on her face. "Hello, I came to get my chair."

"Hi. It's good to see you again." He winked at her. "Please come in. I put your chair upfront." He pointed to it.

"I love it even more than when I first saw it. It's a beautiful piece of furniture. I might never sit in it but instead just admire it."

"You get to do whatever you want with it."

"And here's my check for $600. I made it out to The House of David. If you'd rather have it made out directly to you, I can easily re-write it."

"No, The House of David will be fine. Thank you very much."

He whispered to her, "On Friday morning I'll be looking forward to your Uber call. I'll be driving around the area in the 8-9 o'clock time frame, anxiously awaiting."

"I'm still very scared about this."

"So am I but not enough to want to cancel."

"I guess I feel the same way. If you could carry the chair out to the car, I'd certainly appreciate it.

"I'd be most happy to." He picked up the chair and followed her out the door.

Walking along the driveway, she again admired the roses in his garden. "You have such beautiful roses. And your backyard looks so neat and trimmed. Do you do all of that?"

"I can't afford to pay anyone else to do it. My wife helps but she mostly does the inside plants and I do the outside ones. It works out quite well."

"I'll pop the rear deck lid open." Her car had plenty of room for the chair.

"That should be fine since it's only going over to Rackleff Avenue."

"You remember my street."

"How could I forget?" He wanted to take her arm and pull her to him.

"I guess I'll be off. It's been nice seeing you again. I'm sure I'll love the chair." She spoke loudly enough in case his wife might be listening.

"If not, please bring it back. I guarantee my work."

"That's great. Good bye."

"Goodbye and thanks for the purchase."

He stood there watching as she got into her car and drove off.

CHAPTER 28

It was a slow week for both Melanie and David. Only four days but those seemed to last forever. David tried to absorb himself in building houses and Melanie spent time at her office, working on a new design project.

On Friday morning, David sat at the breakfast table pretending to eat but wasn't hungry. Just a piece of toast and a cup of coffee. He wanted to dress for the lake but didn't want to look too shabby for Melanie. He made a compromise. Slightly worn jeans, a soft red plaid shirt, white sox and his normal work boots that he always wore at the lake. And he made sure he had his wide-brimmed felt hat as well as his walking shoes.

His fishing pole and discretely, Gary's, were added to the car in case Melanie had the urge to fish. And his tool box, in case he had time to do a few upkeep projects, which he was hoping he wouldn't. His things had to be somewhat hidden when he picked up Melanie. Someone might be walking by and wonder why fishing gear was in the rear of an Uber car.

. . .

Melanie was very nervous but tried hard not to show it. She'd spoken with Paul briefly before he headed out the door. He noticed her uneasiness and commented. "You seem to be jumpy this morning. You're not your usual calm self."

"Do I show it? I guess I'm jumpy about my talk. But I think

I'm pretty well prepared. I'll be okay."

"Just try to think of other things to get your mind off of it."

"I'll do that. Thanks for the suggestion." She had no problem with that.

She dressed in her gray business suit along with low black leather heels, an outfit she often wore when going to the New York. Her small suitcase was standing near the front door, but as soon as Paul and the kids left, she added her walking shoes, a pair of gloves, and a wide-brimmed tan hat. Also, some mixed nuts and cookies as well as a bar of fudge for a treat, and two bottles of wine, a Zinfandel and a Chardonnay. She didn't know what else to bring but David seemed to like having wine at their lunch meetings. She still couldn't refer to their escape as a date, even though she knew it was.

It was 7:30. About the time she'd be going to the airport so she texted David. She didn't want to phone him in case he was still at home.

He replied that he would arrive in about a half-hour and said he'd text her again when he was almost there.

Her suitcase was near the front door. She went into the kitchen and had a slice of toast with peanut butter, along with orange juice and a cup of coffee. David said they'd be stopping at Starbucks in Albany so she'd most-likely have a mocha, but she still wanted her morning coffee.

■ ■ ■

David went out to his shop to make sure everything was in order, but mostly to kill time since it only took fifteen minutes to get to Melanie's. He wondered whether he was more excited or more nervous.

He decided to leave in five minutes so he went into the house to say goodbye to Ginny. "I got an Uber call so I'll do that before I head for Moosehead Lake. The extra cash might help."

"As long as you haven't filled up the back seat so you'll have room for the passengers."

"I haven't. I'll say goodbye and be off." He gave her a hug and a peck on the cheek and headed out the door.

CHAPTER 29

David arrived at Melanie's house just after eight.

As soon he approached and stepped onto her porch, the beautiful wood door opened.

"My Uber driver is right on time. I have a small carry-on suitcase if you'd like to help me with it."

"It's my pleasure." He grabbed the bag and moved down the stairs to the walkway, with Melanie following.

She was dressed very smartly in her 'work clothes' but unfortunately no skirt. She was wearing a dark gray business suit and a scarf around her neck. He'd seen her wearing that the first time he picked her up. She had on black leather low heels and carried a small black purse with a strap over her shoulder. Very business-like and attractive. "And I get to spend a weekend with her?" he muttered to himself.

He placed her suitcase on one side of the rear seat and motioned her to the other where he rushed to open her door.

"Thank you, sir."

"You're most welcome. To the Jetport, I presume."

"That's correct."

He closed the door, walked around to his side, climbed in, and they were off.

"Do you think I need to drive to the airport before we do our diversion or should we just head out?"

"No one's home at my house so I think we're safe, although

I'm not sure I'm safe with you. Not your problem. Just mine."

"OK. I'll head out Woodland Street to Baxter Boulevard which should get us to I-295 North."

"You're the Uber driver so I assume you know what you're doing."

"Don't always count on that."

They glanced at each other, smiling.

"Are you nervous, because I definitely am."

"Yes. But we'll relax when we get to the cabin. I think doing anything out of our normal routine can give us anxiety. That's Dr. Stevens talking."

"Doctor, huh. What's your specialty?"

"Getting into trouble."

She laughed. "Well you certainly accomplished that this time."

Sixty-five miles per hour was the speed limit on I-295 North, so David set his cruise control at 70. The road passed through rolling hills with lower regions exposing unique rock outcroppings.

They soon stopped at a roadside rest so Melanie could change out of her business suit. She carried a small bag into the women's restroom and entered a stall, hanging her bag on the door hook. Soon she had her business pants off, replacing them with tan crops. Then came her blouse. After removing it, she hesitated regarding her bra. Should she take it off, or not? She usually had it off at home. And she remembered that David saw her bra-less when he brought the earring to her. Why not take it off? He'd probably never notice. So off it came and on went a soft yellow cotton long sleeve t-shirt. The weather was nice for this time of the year but she wasn't sure about Moosehead Lake.

As she headed to the car she felt refreshed after getting out of her 'work' clothes. Tossing the small bag onto the back seat and carefully laying her suit on top of it, she slid into the front passenger seat.

Normally the t-shirt was loose and un-revealing, but not when she slid into her seat. David definitely took notice.

Soon they were on a large gray arched bridge crossing over the rushing waters of the Presumpscot River in Falmouth. Next came Yarmouth with an old grist mill on their left as they crossed the Royal River.

As they moved further north, the roadsides gradually turned to green forested rural land. They soon came to Freeport, the shopping mecca of the northeast including the world-renowned 100-year old L.L. Bean Store. The entire town could be called a discount outlet as it housed outlets for most of the well-known stores in the country. But they didn't dare stop to shop for fear of running into Portland residents.

David turned on his radio and switched it to the CD player. He had an Eagles CD that began to play *Take It Easy*.

"I figured that might be a good message for us."

"Good choice. I've always loved the Eagles, even though they're before my time."

"Me too. So what kind of music do you like?

"Actually, I like all kinds, from classical to country western. How about you?

"I like all kinds too. I got to hear classical when I was growing up and liked it a lot but I hear mostly country-western at work. That's what the workers play on the job and I get used to it. And Ginny is not really into music."

"Neither is Paul."

"It's probably only another 15 minutes to Starbucks in Brunswick."

"Are you thinking off having your usual mocha? And something to go with it? Notice I said 'usual' but I've only been with you at Starbucks twice and two other times without you. You certainly got me into drinking mochas.

"Definitely a mocha and possibly that wonderful coffee cake. What about you?"

"In the Portland store I saw a blueberry scone that looked good. I'll try that, if they have it."

When they reached Gurnet Road and saw the familiar green and white logo on the building, they pulled up and climbed out, Melanie not waiting for David's personal service this time. She was too anxious for a mocha.

By now Melanie was comfortable with the Starbucks routine and they moved quickly to the ordering line. "I think we should sit together at the window counter," Melanie said. "I'm feeling a little risqué."

"If you're up for it, so am I."

When their turn came, they placed their orders with a young man wearing a green apron, a white shirt, and a black bow tie. Very sharp-looking. They paid for their orders, thanked him and moved to the serving line, holding hands along the way and smiling at each other while their other hands held the treats wrapped in small brown paper bags. When their drinks came, they headed for the service table to collect straws and napkins since they knew the treats would be messy.

Sitting at the window counter, they were experiencing a feeling of freedom, sharing the moment together.

David, the furniture designer, enjoyed rubbing his fingers over the shiny wood counter while sipping his mocha, presuming it was finished with a high-gloss polyurethane. Why was he interested in that? Something to temporarily get his mind off of the risk they were taking?

"I guess I've become even more attached to Starbucks since meeting you on Fridays. It always cheers me up to walk into one."

"I don't have the experience with them that you do but I know the feeling. Look at all the people who seem to be happy."

"It's a great break from what probably is their relatively mundane day."

"It certainly is for me today!"

"Me too." He smiled and took her hand.

Once back on I-295, they'd soon merged with I-95. In a little over an hour they arrived in Pittsfield , a small town of just over 4,000 people, located on the Sebasticook River. A sports-oriented town with snow-mobiles in the winter and mountain biking in the summer and many parks within the town limits. At that point they turned off I-95 and soon came to Palmyra, another popular recreation area of about 2,000 residents.

"Notice how the trees are different when we get further north. Red maples where we live, but up here more red spruce. Beautiful patches of them growing along the roadside, but providing very little shoulder for emergency stopping."

"There's something intriguing about it. Almost like driving down a narrow passageway."

"Yes, like we're heading into another world, at least that's what I imagine I'm doing with you."

Signs directed them to Moosehead Lake on Highway 152 and then 150, arriving at Dover-Foxcraft, originally two logging towns separated by the Piscataaquis River. According to a roadside sign, they were home of the famous Maine Whoopie Pie Festival in the summer.

Then onto Highway 6 North, leading them to Greenville, the town at the south end of Moosehead Lake where the Indian Hill Trading Post was located. When they arrived, they noticed the sign above the store indicated it was a Shop'n Save grocery outlet.

"We'd better stop and get some food for tonight as well as breakfast, since I didn't dare bring anything from the house. "

"Ginny put a few things in the chest for me. I think some bread and butter, a few eggs, and some apples and oranges. And a box of Raisin Bran. I felt guilty about her doing that. So what should we have for dinner tonight?"

"What kind of cooking facilities do you have in your cabin?"

"There's an old coal-fired potbelly stove that you have to stoke up every 15 minutes."

"Really?"

"No. Just kidding. It's a small electric stove with an oven. And a small refrigerator. But how about just having hamburgers on the grill. I'll get my Weber ready. And lettuce, sliced pickles, red onion, and ketchup. I could slice some potatoes lengthwise and grill them along with the burgers. Corn on the grill would also be good."

"I'll make a small salad with lettuce, carrots, celery and maybe some tomatoes if they look good. And I'll get a bottle of salad dressing. What kind do you prefer?"

"My favorite is blue-cheese but I'll take anything."

"That's interesting because that's my favorite also."

They pulled up to the store, with shopping lists in their minds."

Melanie noticed the store had a very complete line of food items as well as wine and liquor. Even the fruit and vegetables looked relatively fresh. They grabbed shopping carts and went their separate ways, Melanie getting the fruits and vegetables and David the meat, bacon, eggs, hamburger buns and bread. They soon met at the register. Melanie noticed that David also had a bottle of red wine in his cart. It looked like a good one, a J Lohr Cabernet Sauvignon.

"I'm impressed that you picked out a nice bottle of red wine."

"I got some help from a man shopping the wine aisle," he said a little sheepishly."

"We're dividing the bill in half. I brought enough cash since I don't want a record of this."

"I didn't think of doing that but Ginny knows I'm up here so a grocery charge on my credit card isn't out of line."

"That's fine with me."

"He turned to the checker and said, "Please put half of this on my card and the other half, cash."

"I can do that," she replied as she bagged the groceries.

They went out to the car pushing a shopping cart in front

of them. The groceries went on the back seat, where there was now plenty of room. David backed the car out and headed up Highway 6.

CHAPTER 30

The drive was very picturesque. Beautiful trees most of the way with occasional glimpses of the lake and its sandy beaches and sharp rock-lined cliffs. It took them a half hour to get to David's turnoff.

Melanie noticed David beginning to slow down.

"Are we there."

"Yes, my road is just ahead."

When they made the turn, Melanie said, "Did you say road? It looks more like a dirt path surrounded by a dense forest, and hasn't been used for years."

"That's all the road I need to get in and out. I hope you weren't expecting a fancy driveway. That would have cost thousands of dollars and also wouldn't be anywhere near as rustic."

"I wasn't complaining, just surprised. I really didn't know what to expect."

Making their way through the trees, Melanie saw a little log cabin and beyond that, the lake. It looked very private and exciting. She noticed a nice-looking door centered in the middle of the cabin along with a window on either side, and attractive logs alternately overlapping at the corners, for strength. The peaked roof included a rib-style metal roof, presumably for when it snowed.

"It's so cute."

"I didn't really build it to be cute, but if that's what you want to call it, that's fine with me."

"I didn't mean cutesy. More picturesque cute. Do you know what I mean."

"I got it."

By then he'd pulled up to a graveled parking area in front. She also noticed small graveled paths leading around the sides of the cabin. A few azaleas were planted in front, and a black wrought iron lamp hung above the entryway, adding charm.

"I was thinking this looks professionally built, but then I realize it was."

"Thank you for the compliment. I take pride in what I build, as you might know by now."

"I definitely do." He had raised the rear deck lid of the CRV and began to unload when she approached him from behind, put her arms around him, and gave him a big hug.

"Wow, where did that come from?"

"Just from little old me, your personal graphic designer."

"I can imagine a lot of things you could design for the weekend. Especially one of those hugs now and then."

"It's a deal. And my rates are very reasonable.

They went inside. The kitchen was to the left and the living room to the right. A large orange and brown shag rug covered the area in front of a beautiful stone fireplace. Opposite that was an L-shaped brown couch covered with decorative pillows, inviting her to curl up. One section faced the fireplace and the other faced the front window. Above the attractive wood fireplace mantle she noticed a beautiful print in a gold frame that had a view of a small cove expanding towards a lake. It must have been taken from the cabin she presumed. A large oak coffee table piled with a few magazines was in front of the couch. She could imagine herself lounging on the couch with a pillow behind her back, staring at a roaring fire.

"This is very warm and cozy. Is that a word I'm allowed to use?"

"You can use any words you want, as long as they're not cuss words. I try to keep those out of my repertoire, except when I pound my finger with a hammer."

A small wood table and four chairs were in the middle of the kitchen. Across from them, the kitchen sink faced one of the front windows. Cupboards lined both the walls above and below the Formica kitchen counters. They were a beautiful natural wood, finished with a cherry stain. Melanie could imagine herself either cooking or sitting at the table having a cup of coffee.

"A very nice look for a cabin. You have good taste, or was this interior designed by your wife?"

"I did it. From a graphic designer I take that as a compliment."

"What about the rest of your place? I see three closed doors. Should I take a guess?"

"Please do."

"I would guess that there are two bedrooms separated by a bathroom. That guess was based upon an earlier discussion."

"You are correct and win the $50,000 prize! Please feel free to have a look."

She opened the door on the right to see a room with white walls and a queen-sized bed with a flowered quilt. Matching pillows were propped up against the headboard. "Those pillows are inviting me to test them out," which she did.

A small closet was located near the door. Next to it was a cherry-colored wood chest of drawers. A chair was near a large double window and a brown shag carpet stretched out in front of the chest. The window was surrounded by white curtains, at this point held to the side by hooks.

She walked over to the window and could see the lake. The property had obviously been cleared of trees to provide an unobstructed view. Melanie thought she could even see the other side of the lake.

"And I might get to sleep here tonight," she said.

"If you're lucky. And if I'm unlucky," he joked.

"Watch your language. Moving on to the middle door, it should be the bathroom."

Opening the door to the narrow room, on one side she saw a vanity with a sink, and a toilet next to it. On the other was a bathtub with a shower. A cupboard near the door probably served as a linen closet. She noticed that the small window at the rear was high enough to provide privacy, even when the flowered plastic window curtain was moved to the side. The room walls were painted with a white, semi-gloss paint and the floor was covered with a gray simulated-tile linoleum.

"A very adequate bathroom."

"I hope it's adequate because that's all we have."

"Oh, I wasn't critiquing it. Just suggesting that it has what we need."

"On to the last door."

"Yes, it has to be a bedroom because you told me there were two."

"The lady guessed correctly." He opened the door.

It had a layout similar to the other bedroom with the bed on the outside wall. A plain cotton bedspread covered the bed with two pillows stacked against the headboard. A small closet was located on the wall next to the bathroom. Near that was a chest. To the right, a small table that could serve as a desk, and a chair under the window. The walls were off-white as in the other rooms, and a small brown and yellow shag rug was in front of the bed.

"That's the house tour. I hope you're happy with it because that's all you get when hanging out with a carpenter."

"I think I can manage."

"We should bring in our stuff. Why don't you grab the groceries and I'll bring in the luggage?"

"That sounds fine with me."

David distributed the bags in their bedrooms while Melanie piled the groceries on the kitchen table. When David returned to the kitchen, Melanie had most of them spread out, wondering where he liked to keep them.

"I'll tell you the way we usually do it but first let me turn on the fridge. I'll also turn on the propane and try one of the stove burners."

"Good idea. We'll certainly need those unless we want to camp out."

"You mean we're not camping out?"

"I guess I would call it refined camping, but it is very exciting."

David showed her where they kept things and soon everything was put away.

"What's next on your agenda, Mr. Stevens?"

"I'd love to show you around the property. There's a lot to see."

"That sounds good to me. Let me put on my sneakers and I'll be ready in a minute." She went into her bedroom, noticing how neatly he'd placed her things on the bed.

She unpacked a few items, hung up her business suit in the closet, and sat down on the chair to put on her sneakers. As she went back to the living room, she grabbed her wide-brimmed Tilley hat that had an airflow opening around the top. Perfect for camping.

In the living room, David was sweeping the floor. "We have a small vacuum cleaner that I'll get out later but I'm just getting some of the dust up. It's obviously been a while since someone was here."

"I'd be glad to do that. Isn't that a woman's job?"

"Not at my house. I believe in equal tasks for men and women. Well, not quite. There are a few differences." He smiled.

"I guess we should be grateful for that."

"Let's head out for a look around."

"Sounds good. I'm ready for anything. Well, almost anything."

He didn't dare respond. He opened the back door and they

walked out towards the lake. She noticed a graveled patio next to the house, covered with leaves, and a trail leading out to a picnic area including a table and attached benches. Otherwise the property between the cabin and the lake was mostly overgrown with high grass. David said he'd mow it sometime during the weekend.

"How do you do that?"

"See that shed over there, almost hiding. That's where I keep my tools. Inside is a small John Deere tractor with a mowing deck. It does a good job of cutting the grass."

"Here I was thinking you'd be pushing around a small lawn mower that would take forever."

"To own a place like this you either have to be very wealthy and hire things done, or you need the tools and equipment to do it yourself. And you know which category I'm in."

"I believe I do. It's also nice not to have to depend on others when you need something done."

As they walked closer to the lake, Melanie noticed a pile of very long logs. Perhaps the kind he used to build the cabin, she thought. They were stacked neatly, waiting for a use.

"What do you plan to do with those logs? Build another cabin. Perhaps a guest house for me?" she smiled.

"I'd love to do that. But an immediate use of them would be to build a raft tomorrow that we can take onto the lake and have a picnic lunch."

"You can build a raft out of those logs?"

"I believe so. I'll use rope to tie them together and place a piece of plywood on top for a deck."

"Sounds exciting and fun."

They came to a bench near the water. David encouraged her to sit down for a few minutes and he sat next to her. She could hear the water lapping up on the beach, and a feeling of peace and calm swept over her.

He took her hand, looked at her, and said, "I'm so glad we're here together. When building this place, I never dreamed I could be sitting here with such a beautiful, caring person."

"Maybe you'll get that chance someday."

"It's already happened." He smiled.

When they got up, he led her to a trail that circled the property. Mostly red spruce trees, with the ground covered by a leaf-mulch that crunched under their feet. Soon they finished the circuit and, as she was approaching the front door, she admired the peaceful setting, the picturesque cabin with its bark-stripped logs neatly stacked to form the walls. She was amazed that David had built it.

CHAPTER 31

As they entered the cabin, she glanced around, taking a more thorough look than when they were unloading. What a homey, cozy feeling. The inviting sofa near the fireplace was waiting for someone to snuggle up on it. How could she be so lucky?

They decided to do a house cleaning before they fixed dinner. David got out the small vacuum cleaner, a broom and a dust pan, as well as dusting rags.

Melanie grabbed the rags and began dusting all of the furniture, including in the bedrooms. She decided she'd use a dish rag to wipe the kitchen and bathroom counters. The dishes, being within closed cupboards, wouldn't need washing.

David swept the floors and Melanie used the vacuum. While doing the rug she imagined lying on it with a pillow propped under her head, enjoying a nice fire. She hoped it would get cold enough.

When finished cleaning, they admired their work. Ready for occupancy.

David went to the shed to get the Weber grill. As he headed out the back door, she enjoyed the sexy way he moved. What was she thinking?

She went into the kitchen to slice the onions, pickles, and tomatoes. She cleaned the iceberg lettuce and punched out the core. Everything went into the fridge.

Since it wasn't quite dinnertime, she decided they could use a beer. Pulling two bottles from the fridge, she opened them and carried them to the patio, where David placed the grill. He'd also brought a couple of folding chairs with lift-up side tables from the shed.

"How did you know that's what I wanted?"

"I figured you could use one, after all that cleanup and getting these things out of the shed. Let's sit down and enjoy ourselves. I hope you don't need a glass."

"Definitely not. Real men don't need beer glasses."

She laughed and clicked her bottle with his. This was too good to be true.

"Do you do this with all the girls you bring here?"

"No, I'm afraid not. I'm pretty fussy. But you need to know that I've never done this before and will never do it again, at least not with anyone but you."

"You're so kind. And this is so special."

A flock of Mallard ducks landed on the water close to the shore and began searching for food. Then an orange-breasted Baltimore Oriele appeared on a tree branch nearby.

"I could put out my bird feeder, but since we'll only be here for a couple of days, it wouldn't be fair to get them used to feeding and then leave."

"You're so sensitive about their needs. That's one of the 10 or 15 things I like about you."

"Really. What are the other fourteen?"

"I'll keep that in reserve for a while."

"I wish I had some flowers to put on both the inside and outside tables. Maybe I could get some from the store tomorrow or pick some along the road."

"That would be nice. I love the way you have flowers in your Uber. It sends a nice message about the driver."

"I'm glad you think so. If it had anything to do with you being here, I'll have even a bigger bouquet next time."

"You're too funny."

David finished his beer and went over to the Weber, lighting the coals in the charcoal chimney with a match and a crumpled-up newspaper.

He then went into the kitchen to make the burgers and also got two buns out of the package. They had to buy six but David could justifiably take them home, claiming he had hamburgers twice.

Melanie got the Cabernet from the cupboard and opened it. David didn't have any wine glasses so they used juice glasses. She filled them half full, handed one to David, and they clicked.

"Cheers. Here's to a thrilling but scary weekend."

"I'll definitely drink to both parts of that."

Melanie saw that the outside thermometer indicated 78 degrees, plenty warm to eat outside. She found a white oilcloth in the cupboard with bright red roses printed on it and arranged it on the picnic table, holding it down with rocks. She then gathered a few green stems from the azaleas in the front, arranging them in an empty peanut butter jar she'd found in the pantry. After filling it with water, she placed the arrangement on the table.

Once the briquets were lit, both David and Melanie headed for the kitchen, David slicing the potatoes in lengthwise strips and wrapping the corn in foil, and Melanie putting a salad together. The most important task was refilling their wine glasses.

This wouldn't be their first meal together, but their first one in a casual setting, away from the stresses of every-day life.

David poured the hot coals into the Weber and spread them around. He then slipped the upper grill in place and put the lid on. After the grill heated up he put on the corn, planning to rotate it one quarter turn every 10 minutes. Next came the potatoes, after brushing them with olive oil and sprinkling them with Nature's Seasoning. Then the burgers, adding garlic and onion powder, and salt and pepper.

When he turned the burgers, he put the sliced buns on the grill to warm up. Soon the medium-rare burgers were ready along with the potatoes and corn. He transferred everything to plates, carrying them to the table.

Melanie brought out the salad and the plate of condiments and they sat down, admiring their efforts. By then they had almost run out of wine again so she topped up their glasses.

David picked up his glass and held it towards Melanie, with her following his lead. "Cheers to a beautiful day with a beautiful woman."

"I don't quite know how to follow that but I'll toast to an exciting, sensitive man. And by the way, do we know what we're doing here yet?"

"I don't think so, but if you figure it out, be sure to let me know."

They proceeded to garnish their burgers, and also added ketchup to the browned potatoes. After removing the husks, Melanie buttered her corn but David preferred his without the butter.

They devoured their food, not saying much in the process. They were comfortable just being together.

Melanie was enjoying the view, first of all of the handsome man across from her but also of the surroundings, including the trees, the cleared region surrounding the small cove, and the lake beyond. It made her feel as close to paradise as she could imagine.

"Since you did most of the cooking, I'm doing the cleanup and dishes."

"I'm not happy with you getting stuck with that but I'll help you carry the dishes inside. After you finish, let's take another walk around the property. The sun will be going down and the moon should be out by then."

"A good plan."

After doing the cleanup, Melanie moved to the patio and noticed David returning from the shed.

"I was just checking out the mower and filling the tank with gas. Fortunately, I'd left a canister partially filled last fall. I'm going to mow the grass tomorrow morning either before or after breakfast. But unfortunately, it will be noisy, not the serene setting you have now.

"I love how it looks, but having it mowed will also be great."

"And we're supposed to have great weather most of the time."

"That's good news. But if it were raining and we had to stay inside sitting around a cozy fire, that wouldn't be too bad either."

"Are you ready to walk?"

"I have my walking shoes on. You lead the way."

"Rather than leading, I'd like to walk next to you."

"I'd like that."

They did a slow stroll around the property for about a half hour and returned to the cabin. It was too nice to go inside, so they sat on their patio chairs and admired the sky. The moon was about halfway up from the horizon by then, illuminating the lake and the grassy area in front of them. What an inspiring setting, Melanie decided.

It wasn't long before the wine they'd consumed caught up with them and they both yawned, laughing as they did.

"I guess it must be bedtime. Too warm to sit around a fire. It's been wonderful, but now I'm ready for bed."

"I guess I am, too," David said. "Why don't you use the bathroom first and I'll follow."

"Women take a lot longer than men. You're sure you don't want to go first?"

"No, I'll be fine. I think I'll sit out here while you do your thing and you can let me know when you're finished."

"No sooner said than done."

She went into her bedroom, changed into a pink pajama top and a pink and white flowered robe and went to the bathroom to take care of her nightly routine.

Later, as she came out of the bathroom, David turned his head and looked at her. "You look very sexy."

She was a little startled by his boldness.

"I don't know whether that's a compliment or a come-on."

"Neither. Just an observation."

"If it's a compliment, I thank you." She was glad the subject of bedroom choices hadn't come up. She thought David might have tried to encourage her to spend the night with him, but he was being very cautious. She was glad of that, not that it didn't interest her.

Climbing into bed and pulling the covers up, she turned on her reading light and got out her book. After reading a couple of pages, there was a knock on her door. She hesitated, wondering what was up, but said, "Come in."

David poked his head around the door and said, "I just wanted to say good night to you." He walked over to the bed and said, "Just a good night kiss."

Oh, Oh, she thought. Here it comes.

Instead, he leaned over and kissed her on the cheek. "Sweet dreams."

"Thank you. That was very nice. And sweet dreams to you too."

When he left, she was feeling very content. A great way to end a super day.

CHAPTER 32

When Melanie awakened Saturday morning, her half-opened eyes were looking at a window curtain illuminated by bright sunshine. Where was she? Then she remembered. David's cottage. Thinking of him, she turned over and snuggled her head in the pillow.

After a few moments, she heard some noises coming from the kitchen. She decided David was making coffee. A nice cup of freshly-brewed coffee sounded awfully good.

She threw back the comforter and swung her legs over the side of the bed. "Could I go out there in my pajamas and robe, or should I get dressed first . He saw me last night this way so it should be alright, at least while I have my coffee."

She jumped up, slipped her robe over the pajamas, slid into her slippers, and moved to the bedroom door.

He was standing near the kitchen sink in his boxer shorts, pouring water into the coffee maker. When she walked over to the table and sat down, he turned around and said, "You look beautiful, so comfortable in your robe and slippers. I'll bet you could go for a cup of coffee?"

"How did you guess? Notice I didn't even wait to get dressed."

"I definitely noticed, and I'm glad. I like seeing you undressed. Uh, …I don't mean it that way. I mean in your robe and slippers. You look like you're very refreshed and relaxed," although he certainly wouldn't mind seeing her undressed.

He brought her mug of coffee to the table along with a small Danish pastry from a package they'd purchased at the store. While setting her coffee in front of her, he noticed her robe had separated slightly above her knees. He almost dropped her mug but quickly recovered. A short time later, he topped up her coffee, hoping for another view, but by then the robe was pulled tightly across her legs.

He sat down across from her with his Danish and coffee and took a sip, while looking at her and smiling.

"Welcome to 'Breakfast at Tiffany's' if that's an expression of a great place to have breakfast, because this place might be even better."

"So what's up for breakfast. What can I do?"

"I'd like to make breakfast for you this morning. I'm suggesting French toast and bacon, along with some sliced fruit. How does that sound? I've even got the bacon going on the Weber."

"It sounds wonderful."

"And if you want to participate, I'll let you set the table and pour some juice."

"No sooner said than done. I'll do that right now and then get dressed."

"I like seeing you in your robe but I guess you can't wear that around all day."

"I'm afraid not."

She went to her bedroom and dressed in the same clothes she wore the previous day. Returning to the table, she poured another cup of coffee and pulled up a chair.

"I'm going to enjoy watching you cook."

"That's what I'm here for."

A short time later, while eating, he talked about the kitchen facilities he'd chosen when building the cabin and how much he loved to cook.

"Cooking's relatively unusual for a man. How did it infect you?"

"It was my Mom. She always let me watch her and later she would let me make part of the dinner. I find it very challenging to combine various ingredients and see how they blend together."

"I feel the same way. So maybe you'll let me do dinner tonight. We'll have to go to the store to get some of the ingredients and I hope you'll think the dinner will be worth the drive."

"Driving anywhere with you is worth it. And I'm doing the breakfast dishes. I believe in cleaning up my own mess. I even do that on the job. And after I finish, I'm going to mow the grass. Perhaps you can sit on the patio and watch me work. It will be a pleasant job if I know you're watching."

"I'd love that."

She grabbed her book from the bedroom and migrated to the patio. While sitting in one of the chairs, she heard an engine roar. Soon David and his green John Deere tractor came barreling out of the shed at a reasonably high speed. David was having fun and showing off. He began making the rounds, occasionally diverting into various cutouts until the remaining uncut region was just one large circle.

Melanie waved to him as he circled around, returning his smile.

When finished, he returned the tractor to the shed and ambled back to the patio, sitting down next to Melanie.

"There. Doesn't it look a lot better?"

"Definitely. And it smells so good. Have you thought about what we could do for the rest of the day?"

"I have. That is, if you approve."

"OK. You sound hesitant. Let's have it."

"I'd like to build a raft out of those logs stacked near the water, and take you out for a picnic lunch."

"Are you kidding? You could build a raft that quickly, and it would support both of us?"

"I believe I can."

"I'd certainly love to watch. But it seems like an impossible task."

"I'll give it a try if you promise to have a picnic lunch on it with me if I'm successful."

"It's a deal!"

CHAPTER 33

David headed for the shed wearing old jeans, a long sleeve shirt and work boots. He soon came out with a coil of rope, a knife and a hammer.

"Hey handsome, I hope you're not planning to hang yourself. I wouldn't have anyone to cook dinner for."

"You could always pick up a hitchhiker along the road."

"But I'm pretty fussy."

"In that case, I guess I'll have to build a raft instead of hanging myself."

He put his tools and rope down near the lake, put on a pair of gloves, and walked over to the pile of logs, grabbing one and dragging it near the tools.

At that point, Melanie could see that he was serious about the project so she folded up her chair and carried it to where he was working, placing it down in the shade of a nearby tree. She noticed the smell of freshly-mowed grass was even stronger near the lake.

"I think you need a supervisor so you won't get hurt."

"The only way I'd get hurt is taking my eyes off the job to look at you."

"Are you trying to establish an excuse in case you make a mistake?"

"No. Just talking realistically."

"I find it fascinating watching you, and not just because you're building something."

"How do I interpret that?"

"However you'd like to."

He dragged another log over and laid it next to the first one. Soon he had a dozen of them lined up adjacent to each other.

"I think I'm beginning to envision what you have in mind."

"About the raft, or otherwise?" He smiled.

"I'll let that one go by."

He picked up the rope, tied it to the end of the first log, wrapped it around twice and then onto the next one, and so on, until he had all of the logs tied together on one end. He repeated the process on the other end until he had a dozen logs tied together, creating a flat raft.

"I see what you've done, but where do we sit?"

"You haven't seen the last step yet."

He went over to the shed and slid out a large piece of plywood, dragged it over to the raft, and laid it on top.

Turning to her, he said, "Voila. A useful raft. The plywood doesn't cover the entire raft, but it's enough for us to sit on. Would you care to join me for lunch, floating on the beautiful lake?"

"I guess so, if you guarantee that it won't sink."

"I think I can do that."

"Fine, let's get lunch together, and change into some boating clothes."

"I didn't bring my nautical hat but I'm definitely for the lunch. We have sliced turkey and a good sourdough bread."

They went into the kitchen and got out the sandwich makings. Melanie put two thick turkey sandwiches together on the sourdough bread including mayonnaise, lettuce, tomato, and other trimmings. She wrapped them in plastic wrap, placed them in a small cooler along with two apples, a few cookies, and four Sam Adams beers.

David soon emerged from his bedroom wearing a pair of dark

blue swimming trunks and a white t-shirt. He sat at the table waiting for Melanie, who soon came out in white short shorts and a bright yellow t-shirt. This was the first time he'd seen her in shorts and was overwhelmed by how shapely her legs were. He had a difficult time not staring.

"I guess I'm ready," she said.

"Ready for what?" he joked. "It's going to be difficult to concentrate on paddling with you sitting near me."

"I think you can handle it. You're a big boy."

"We might need a blanket but I don't know how dry it'll be on the raft deck. I have two beach chairs that will keep us dry while we have our lunch."

He gathered the chairs and an old blanket from the shed and carried them to the raft, putting them on the plywood deck along with the cooler. David also brought two paddles and a long wooden pole.

"The lake isn't very deep in this area so I can pole us around, just like in Venice."

"How does a carpenter know about places like Venice?"

"I read a lot and also dream a lot."

"That's obvious to me just being around you. You certainly speak as well as any college graduate I know."

"I guess that's a compliment, although I know a lot of college graduates that don't speak well at all, mainly from my being an Uber driver."

"You're right. I guess I was referring to any well-educated person."

"Enough of tossing out compliments, let's get this show on the road. If you could stand at one end of the raft and I'll be on the other, I think we can easily shove this creature into the water. I hope you're wearing sandals that can get wet."

"I am. So let's go!"

The raft slid relatively easily through the sand and mud into the water.

"Jump on! Here we go."

While Melanie climbed on, David remained in the water to push the raft out farther.

Melanie was soon stretched out on the blankets propped up on her elbows, watching David while he poled the raft away from the beach. She was admiring his muscular body.

David occasionally glanced at her and at times, when she was looking across the lake, he admired the short shorts she was wearing. They were definitely not the tight-fitting type.

Suddenly Melanie let out a loud scream.

She had pulled her legs up to her chest and was panicked.

"Did that poor little snake scare you?" A snake had poked its head up between two of the logs and was looking around. "It's just a little water snake. It won't hurt you. You probably scared him more than he scared you."

David reached down and grabbed the snake by the neck, and in doing so, couldn't help notice the gap that had occurred in Melanie's shorts, revealing her panties as well as a small patch of fuzz. He immediately turned his head towards the lake, jumped up, and tossed the snake into the water.

"There, does that calm you down?"

"Yes, it definitely does." As he was standing up, she noticed a slight bulge in his trunks that wasn't helping calm her down.

David immediately turned away to hide his embarrassment.

They moved farther out into the lake until David decided they were in a good place to have a beer. He didn't know whether to sit opposite her, for another view, or sit next to her to prevent an increase in his blood pressure.

After setting up the chairs, he took two beers from the cooler, popped them open, and handed one to her.

Sitting there, they sipped while the raft drifted slowly around, providing a great view of the shoreline as well as the sun reflecting off the small wavelets in the bright blue water.

"Is this called paradise?" Melanie said.

"If not, it's pretty darned close."

"Are you getting hungry?"

"I am. Let's get out the food!"

Melanie spread a dishtowel between them to serve as a table-cloth and got out the lunch. They had no trouble devouring the sandwiches and chomping on their apples. They were soon having their second beer.

"Just think. If you had a cost-effective furniture manufacturing business, you could have it here."

"I certainly could make the pieces here but it's pretty far from humanity to be able to sell any of it. I'd need a showroom someplace where there were lots of people, and that would require another person to run the showroom. I couldn't afford to do any of that and feed my family."

"You have to think big. But I guess you would still have to show your furniture to sell it. I can't imagine buying a specially designed piece of furniture on line. The buyer would want to see it."

"That's true but I have sold a few pieces by people looking at a sketch along with a detailed written description."

"You just don't know how the business would work unless you try."

"But it's difficult to know where to begin."

"Changing the subject, those beers have made me feel a bit sleepy. Do you suppose we could have a short nap before we return to the cabin? It's so peaceful out here."

"There's certainly no harm in doing that. I probably won't sleep but I'm very content sitting next to you. I'll be thinking about furniture designs. You make me feel creative."

"You've definitely been creative around me."

After a brief nap, Melanie awakened to find David looking at her. "What are you looking at?"

"Just you. How beautiful you are. And how lucky I am being able to sit next to you."

"You keep saying that. It makes me feel like I should try out for Miss America, although it would have to be Mrs. America. Oh, I'm sorry I brought the marriage thing up. Such thoughts could put a damper on this wonderful weekend."

David stood up and began poling them back to shore. Melanie could see he was very competent with the pole in not only propelling them, but also in steering.

When the raft reached shore, they jumped off and pushed it onto the beach. As before, it slid quite easily over the soft mud and sand.

Melanie stood there for a moment, observing the raft. "You're a very clever person to build this raft in a couple of hours. I had a wonderful time riding on it. Thank you." She gave him a peck on the cheek.

"Wow! That made the whole project worthwhile."

After carrying the chairs and blanket to the shed, they were walking back to the cabin when Melanie spoke up: "I just remembered that we have to go to the store to get food for dinner."

"You're right. I guess we were having too much fun. Let's jump in the car and head south."

CHAPTER 34

Melanie had a pencil and paper on her lap while David drove. "Since it's my turn to cook tonight, I get to decide the menu. I'm going to fix spaghetti with meat sauce along with garlic bread and a salad. How does that sound?"

"Wonderful. Anything you cook would be wonderful."

"It sounds like you're an easy man to please."

"With you, yes."

The store had a small meat counter where she was able to get fresh ground beef. She selected a box of spaghetti and a loaf of French bread and vegetables for a salad. For dessert, she chose a pint of Ben & Jerry's Cherry Garcia ice cream. She hoped he would like it and also hoped it wouldn't melt before they got back to the cabin. The bottle of red wine from her suitcase would go good with the spaghetti.

"David, I'm ready to check out."

"OK. Go ahead. I'll meet you up front."

He must be planning something special, she decided.

She thought of the ice cream melting so she decided to ask the grocery checker if she could leave it in the freezer until they were ready to leave. He readily agreed.

David soon arrived to check out, shielding his purchases. He caught up with her after his items were bagged.

As they started to exit, the grocery clerk called to her. "Did you forget something?"

"Oh yes. Thank you for reminding me."

She rushed to the freezer, took out the ice cream and got a double bag from the clerk for insulation.

When they arrived at the cabin it was nearly 6 p.m. Time to start dinner. They unpacked their groceries, putting things in the fridge as necessary, with David making sure his were hidden, and Melanie getting the Ben & Jerry's in the freezer, also hidden.

Melanie uncorked a bottle of wine, pouring glasses for both of them.

"A strong guy like you needs to recover from all that hard work you did. Do you realize that you hauled logs in the morning and then poled me around the lake during lunch time. That takes a lot of energy. You must be worn out."

"No. With you around I'm operating on adrenaline. But I'll certainly be glad to take that glass of wine."

Melanie heated a frying pan and added the chopped ground beef, sliced yellow onion and three cloves of garlic. Adding a can of tomatoes and salt and pepper, she let it cook for 15 minutes.

The pasta was next along with a lettuce, tomato, red pepper and celery salad. Coating the bread with butter and sprinkling the slices with chopped garlic, she put them into the oven. When the bread was done, dinner was ready.

David was already sitting in his chair enjoying the wine when Melanie served him. "I hope this will re-energize you."

"For what? What did you have in mind?"

"Just having you get back the energy you used up earlier." although that's not what she was thinking.

After finishing dinner, and finishing the bottle of wine, David suggested they take a walk around the property, as they did the previous night.

"Maybe I should put on some warmer clothes."

"I think it's warm enough. You'll be fine."

"I'll take your word for it. And I have a surprise dessert for us when we get back."

"I hope it's what I'm thinking of," he said as he smiled.

She didn't catch the implication and said, "I'm not sure what you were hoping but I think you'll like what I have."

"I'm sure I will."

They held hands while walking on the trail around the property, enjoying the stillness of the evening and the birds tweeting.

When they arrived back at the cabin, David said, "How would you like to have a nice fire in the fireplace to finish the evening, after we have this magical dessert?"

"That sounds great to me"

"Okay, I'll get it going while we're eating."

After setting the logs and lighting the fire, he returned to the kitchen,

"Sit down at the table so I can serve you."

"Yes Ma'am."

She got out the ice cream from the freezer, trying to keep it hidden while dishing it up, and then placing a bowl of it in front of David.

"This is one of my favorite dessert."

He took a spoonful and exclaimed, "I love it. What flavor is it?"

"It's Ben & Jerry's Cherry Garcia, named after you know who."

"Well, here's to both Jerry's, the namesake and the one who made it."

After finishing, David tended the fire while Melanie washed the dishes.

CHAPTER 35

After drying and putting away the dishes, they moved to the living room. He'd placed a few fluffy white pillows on the rug for their heads.

Standing in front of the warm fire with his arm around her he was looking at her profile while she was absorbed in watching the mysterious flames, and appreciating the warmth they radiated. "You surprised me with that wonderful dessert. Now I'd like to surprise you with a fantastic drink," he said as he kissed her cheek.

She turned her face towards him, smiling. "That sounds exciting. What's in it?"

"I'll tell you after you've had a sip. I'll put some music on so we can listen while I'm fixing your drink. Is classical okay?"

"I thought you said you usually listened to country music."

"That's when I'm in a work environment. I get to hear that all day so I get used to it. But in a setting like this, nothing beats Beethoven or Mozart. This is Beethoven's piano sonata number 14, the Moonlight Sonata. I'm sure you're familiar with it."

"It's one of my favorites." He seems to know so much about classical music, she realized.

He soon brought her a small glass containing a dark-colored drink on ice. They raised their glasses, their faces near each other, and clicked them.

She took a sip. "I love this. What is it?"

"I'll reveal it now that I know you like it. It's brandy with a little Triple Sec and Kahlua. Something I made up, with some experimentation."

"It's wonderful. Can I call it a David cocktail."

"I'll go for that," he said as he took a sip.

"Do you mind if I ask how a person who grows up in a relatively uneducated family, and works as a carpenter, learns to enjoy some of the finer things in life?"

"My family is certainly relatively poor and uneducated, in terms of having degrees, but my mother loves to cook and they've always enjoyed classical music. I've never heard it played live, but I love it."

"That's a great story. I wish we could go to a concert together but I don't think that's in the cards."

"You're right. So why don't we just lie on the rug and enjoy the fire and listen to the music?"

"I'm certainly up for that."

They laid down on the pillows and Melanie closed her eyes. This was too good to be true. He likes the things I like.

The next piece was Beethoven's violin concerto, another very romantic piece.

"You certainly know how to charm a girl."

"I'm trying."

She slid her pillow over towards him, snuggled her head into his neck and reached her arm across his chest. The smoke from the fire, a well as the masculine scent and freshly mown grass smell coming from him were very stimulating. It was mesmerizing.

He reached his arm under her neck and undid her pony tail clasp so that her hair flowed around her face. Raising up, he looked at her and began stroking her cheeks while gently pushing her hair back behind her ears. At that point she had her eyes closed.

"I like you with your hair down."

They lay there for a while, enjoying the music. Then Beethoven's piano sonata number 8, the Pathetique, began to play.

He leaned over and kissed her behind her ear and whispered, "I'm so glad I met you."

At that point, Melanie couldn't hold back any longer. She did what she'd wanted to do for two days. She pulled herself up and moved her face over to match his and covered his lips with hers. He put his arms around her and pulled her as close as he could. The embrace lasted for several minutes with them exploring each other's lips and tongues.

Finally, Melanie pulled away, moved over onto her back, and looked up at the ceiling.

He noticed the dreamy look on her face.

Suddenly she moved on top of him and began kissing him again. As their lips joined, she felt part of his body become active. It was an exciting feeling.

When she raised her head, David looked at her and placed his hands on her breasts, carefully stroking them and touching her nipples through the fabric.

She let out a soft moan, while rotating her hips. At the same time his hands reached behind her and pressed her to him.

He took hold of her shirt and her breasts appeared as he raised it up.

Pushing her hair back behind her ears, he pulled her lips towards his.

She'd never been aggressive with any man. She had always been the one to follow, not to lead.

She raised up and slid her shorts off, revealing her pink panties."

"Now it's your turn Mister. Let's see what you've got."

He was happily shocked to have her direct this adventure, so he slid his shorts down around his knees.

"Wow. I think you pass the test."

"What test?"

"Being ready for an adventure."

She slid her panties down revealing a golden tuft of hair.

She carefully took their remaining clothing off and moved back on top of him.

Supporting herself above him by her elbows, she could feel him stirring and began circulating her body while he glided his fingers over her naked back and then her breasts. When she couldn't stand it any longer, she encompassed him while letting out a moan.

A dance began with several minutes of slow movement, the pace finally picking up until they climaxed together.

She fell on top of him and they circled their arms around each other, hoping this feeling would never end. He continued to caress the soft skin on her back, occasionally moving his hands around to her breasts.

They soon fell asleep.

After a short while, David awoke and was admiring her body, but didn't feel right about seeing her lying there naked. He got up and grabbed a blanket from the sofa, draped it over her and gently picked her up, carrying her to his bedroom, laying her on the bed. She awoke and smiled and then went back to sleep. Unable to resist, he partially uncovered her and ran his fingers slowly over her body while she occasionally moaned.

What did she see in him, he wondered? He was just a lowly carpenter who played around with furniture designs. Was he missing something? With her attractiveness and charm, if she wanted to have an affair she could choose any man in Portland. Why him? How could he be that lucky?

A couple of hours later, Melanie woke up to feel David's hand caressing her face and her breasts. Eventually it ended up between her legs, slowly stroking her while she moaned with pleasure. She had to be dreaming. Nothing could feel that good.

He put his mouth on her nipples, playing with them until they again became very enlarged and hard. He then softly kissed her forehead and her neck.

"That was so wonderful," she said. "I never thought I could experience anything like it."

She lowered her hand to his groin and, while stroking him, she said, "I think it might be your turn to be on top."

He climbed over her and began moving his hips side to side while rubbing against her. After entering, they both came rather quickly.

As the night continued they slept for a while, made love, and then went back to sleep, the cycle lasting until they fell asleep around 6 a.m.

CHAPTER 36

They slept until 9 a.m. David woke up first and was looking at Melanie curled up next to him, her hand on his chest, sleeping very contentedly. How could anything be as wonderful as last night, he thought?

Her eyes blinked open.

"Hi beautiful."

"Good morning," she said. "Did I die and go to heaven?"

"I'm afraid not. But I think we might have found heaven on earth."

"We must still be there." she said as she reached for him. "Oh, I definitely think we are."

They began a dance, softly caressing each other over their entire bodies. Losing track of time, they acted as though they were not in this world.

When David entered her, they began making slow movements. When they finished they decided they needed to do something else or they'd wear themselves out, especially the moving parts.

"My turn to make breakfast," she said. "That is, if I can concentrate long enough."

She slipped out of bed, pulled on her short nightgown, and headed for the kitchen.

Inserting both the filter and the coffee into the pot, she added water and pushed the button. Not quite as easy as her Keurig but it would be good.

She got out bacon, eggs, and milk. After getting the bacon cooking, she whipped together the ingredients for an omelet and poured the mixture into a large non-stick pan. Carefully pushing up the edges of the mixture, she soon had a bubbly omelet. She flipped half of it over and let it continue to cook, finally placing it on David's plate along with the bacon. She repeated the process for herself.

"For some reason sitting across from you is not quite as enjoyable as being next to you. I can't touch you," he said.

"You'll get plenty of chances for that."

"I hope so."

They finished eating and sat there while enjoying a second cup of coffee.

"Is last night anything like running a marathon?" she amusingly said.

"I've only run one once but as far as energy output, that came pretty close."

Melanie was thinking about how quickly she had become intimate with a man she'd only known for a few weeks. That was not how she normally behaved. It had always taken quite a while before she became intimate with a man, but those experiences never came close to what had happened during the night. Even with her husband, it was at least several months before they became intimate. She couldn't seem to control herself with David.

"What's on our agenda for today, besides the indoor activities?" she said.

"I have a suggestion that I think you'd like."

"Try me."

"Do you like raspberries?"

"I love them. One of my favorite fruits."

"There are a lot of wild raspberry bushes growing along the logging roads near here. We could drive there and pick the berries. They would provide us with a nice fruit salad, or even a dessert if we mash them and have them over ice cream."

"That sounds like fun. Let's do it. I have to cleanup and do the dishes. When were you thinking of going?"

"How about in a half hour? I've got a few odd jobs that I'll quickly take care of or Ginny would wonder what I'd accomplished while I was here."

"We certainly wouldn't want that to happen."

She wasn't used to having to wash dishes since she'd always had access to a dishwasher, but she was enjoying the scrubbing, rinsing, and drying. She liked leaving the kitchen very neat.

While she watched David repairing the walls of the shed, she was leaning against the sink and having to move to keep him in her view. In doing so, she became aware that her lower body was quite sensitive to the movement. She couldn't remember anything like that happening before. Maybe she should address the issue before they went raspberry picking.

Later, David came in with dirty jeans as well as dirty hands and face.

In a bold move, Melanie approached him and said, "I'm going to clean you up. Let's head for the shower."

His eyes lit up. "Really. You mean you and I will shower together?"

"I thought that's what I said." She smiled and grabbed his hand. "Let's go."

She led him into the bathroom and began undressing him. First his shirt, then his jeans, and finally his shorts. "I think some work needs to be done down here, but I'll wash you all over first."

He reached around her with both hands and pulled her towards him. Her nightgown pressed against his sweaty chest as they experienced a long kiss.

She turned on the water and while it was warming up, she did a quick undressing and got ready to climb into the tub. She grabbed David's naked hips, partially to steady herself while stepping over the edge of the tub but also to admire his rear end.

Pulling the light blue shower curtain closed, she switched on the shower faucet and drowned them both in the spray, while they laughed. She began scrubbing David from head to toe, spending a little extra time below his chest and then turning him around for a rinse.

I believe you missed something," David said.

"What was that?"

He reached his hands behind her, grabbed her bottom and carefully lifted her onto him. They remained almost motionless for several minutes, the soft warm water engulfing them while they kissed. Melanie tousled his hair with her fingers and then rubbed his back, very much enjoying their union.

David moved her side to side, with his strong hands grasping her rear end in a massaging motion. That movement soon brought results.

"I'll bet that's what you had in mind while you were washing me," he said.

"I'm not that kind of a girl." She smiled.

"Whatever you are, you've got me totally under your power."

"You forgot to wash me."

"You didn't get dirty but I'd love to do it." He scrubbed her gently, especially in certain areas. It turned out to be a fairly complete massage with Melanie closing her eyes and appearing to be dreaming. When the water finally became cool, he turned it off and they grabbed towels, each drying the other.

"Now I'm ready to pick raspberries."

"Will we get dirty again so can we have another shower?"

"Not a bad idea. "

CHAPTER 37

David dressed in jeans and a burgundy-colored t-shirt while Melanie wore a tan shirt and denim culottes. They took several wide plastic-lid containers, not wanting to pile the raspberries too high for fear of getting them smashed. They soon headed out of David's long driveway and turned north.

After about 10 miles, David began slowing down, looking intently for a partially obstructed narrow dirt road. He finally saw it and made a left turn, passing through some tree branches overhanging the path. They then bumped along for another 5 miles until they came to an open grassy field where he pulled to the side and parked. They could see the berry bushes ahead of them, clustered along the path.

After putting on their hats, they were anxious to begin picking.

"Look at the raspberries. Thousands of them!"

"They're all ours for the taking."

"How do you know they're not owned by someone? We might be stealing."

"I know the people who own this property and they told me I can pick berries anytime."

"Oh. So I guess I can do it also, as long as I'm with you."

"Yes, I'm handy to have around for some things."

"More than just picking berries. I'll certainly attest to that." She smiled.

They approached a large patch and began picking. Melanie put a few in her mouth. "These are fantastic. So sweet."

"They're better than anything you can buy."

Just then, David reached in front of Melanie and pulled her back.

"Keep quiet."

"Why," she whispered.

"There's a black bear approaching. Don't panic. Speak in a calm tone and begin to back up very slowly."

"Anything you say. I've never had a bear approach me before unless he was in a zoo."

The bear soon stopped, looked at them for a few moments, and then turned and ambled away.

"They're not very dangerous. You just don't want to panic them. The grizzly bears are the dangerous ones and they're not typically in our area."

"That was still pretty scary. I'm so glad you knew how to react. Did you just save my life again?"

"No. These bears are looking for food that people leave around on tables or in containers that aren't locked. They're very smart and can figure out how to open trash cans."

"Nevertheless, that was scary. Can we continue picking?"

"Definitely. We have to fill our containers.

The sun disappeared behind clouds, and the sky looked threatening. It wasn't long before it began to rain, but it was so warm, they didn't mind getting soaked. Especially David, since Melanie's breasts became quite visible in her wet t-shirt.

He reached his arm around her waist and pulled her to him, both of them lowering their containers to the ground. After a long kiss, David looked around and saw a small patch of grass next to the path. He swung her down onto it, making sure her hat was under her head.

They lay beside each other, the rain dripping off of their faces. With his hand he pushed the drops off of her while admiring her soft facial skin. He kissed her again and squeezed her breasts through her t-shirt. By then their shirts were soaking wet and her nipples were very visible.

He reached down and undid her pants, sliding them down to her ankles along with her panties. Her genital hair soon became wet, partially from the rain but also from her excitement. He caressed the area, smoothing the raindrops from her soft thighs. His fingers soon found what they were searching for and provided a very strong arousal. Melanie cried out softly until she couldn't stand it anymore.

David slid her t-shirt up above her breasts, placing his lips alternately on each of the enlarged nipples. Then they moved to her mouth where their lips and tongues were soon intertwined.

It wasn't long before Melanie spread her knees apart, welcoming him.

"I hope you don't see any bears," she said.

"I definitely see something bare that I'd like to check out, but no bears."

"I give you full permission. I just hope no one comes along on the trail."

"If they do, they'll get an eye full."

They were soon moving in slow motion but the pace quickened rapidly. The rain was falling on Melanie's face and David's back, but that was the furthest thing from their minds. After they finished their little *tete-a-tete*, they weren't quite sure what to do. David wanted to remain on top of her to protect her from the rain but he knew he couldn't do that forever. He finally pushed himself up, helped Melanie draw her pants up, and pulled her up by her arms.

She stood in front of him and gave him a big kiss.

"That was so romantic and exciting. I wish we could have stripped down completely. Then the rain wouldn't have mattered."

"What we just did was not on my agenda. It was spontaneous, but I'll certainly never forget it. Every time I see a raspberry I might have an orgasm."

"You silly boy," she said as she reached up and pushed his wet hair away from his eyes and gave him another kiss.

"Where do we go from here?" he said.

"I guess we keep picking until our containers are full. I don't mind the rain. And from the looks of the clouds, it will be over soon."

After a short time, the rain stopped and they were back at the CRV, pleased with their harvest. David had a couple of towels in the back which they used to dry off with.

"Quite an outing," she said once she settled into her seat. "Did you order the bear, and the rain, and everything else?"

"I did, indeed. It cost quite a bit but it was definitely worth it."

"I agree."

When they arrived back at the cottage, after putting the raspberries in the fridge, they headed for the bathroom and stripped off their wet clothes, no modesty this time. They were feeling comfortable being naked together. They decided they didn't need another shower. He dried her back, and she, his. Then they turned and had a long embrace with David feeling some activity but deciding he'd better save it for later.

CHAPTER 38

"I was thinking about our adventure. Since I'm a carpenter, could I claim that I nailed you on the trail?"

That's pretty funny, but I guess that's what you did. And I definitely like your tools. You seemed to know what to do with them. And speaking of doing, I was thinking about fixing lunch. We could have tuna sandwiches along with lettuce and tomato."

"Not as good as having you, but I have a better suggestion. Why don't we take a drive north to the little town of Rockwood and have lunch? We could save the tuna sandwiches for tomorrow before we leave."

"Do we really have to leave?"

"You feel the same as I do. It's such a beautiful day and I think you'd enjoy seeing more of the lake and the surroundings. Some of the area is cluttered with cottages but there is also a lot of beautiful vegetation."

"I'd love that. Especially doing it with you, my private tour guide."

"There are no roads that go all the way around the lake. The access is mostly on side roads. It would take us all day to visit those places and already half the day is gone."

"I'm happy just being with you and going where you'd like."

"Okay. If that's settled, there's a little bar and grill, actually called the Rockwood Bar and Grill and guess where it's located??

"Give me a minute. Rockwood? Let's go! That sounds like a

great plan. Should I wear shorts or jeans?"

"You know I love to look at your legs, but wear whatever you think would be comfortable. The bar and grill might be air conditioned so keep that in mind."

'OK. It'll be jeans and a short sleeve shirt."

"That's what I'll wear too."

Melanie kept her clothes in her bedroom although she wasn't planning on sleeping there anymore. In addition to her black jeans, she wore a light blue short-sleeve cotton shirt with only the top two buttons unbuttoned. Even though she and David had been intimate, she was still modest about how she dressed in public. She tied her hair in a ponytail, clipping it with a brown plastic hairpiece, and then put on her grey sneakers with no sox.

David had on blue jeans, a tan t-shirt with Moosehead Lake emblazoned on the front, and sandals with no sox. His blond hair didn't need combing. It was short enough that he brushed it aside.

After locking up the cabin, they climbed into his car and drove slowly along the rutted driveway. When they reached Highway 15, they turned right, heading north towards Rockwood. David explained that this section of the highway was the only part that went near the picturesque lake and would be new territory for Melanie.

During their drive they passed dense green forests and sprawling fields and farmhouses, as well as going over several picturesque stone bridges that crossed rivers that were feeding the lake. But the lake itself was the most inspiring. The beautiful deep blue color. It was being used extensively by boaters, as well as beach-loving people on the few beaches they passed.

They could see they were approaching a small town ahead. "Is this Rockwood?" Melanie asked.

"If you blink while driving through, you'll miss it."

"A charming place. I see the post office, that yellow brick building with the flag in front."

"And up ahead you'll see our destination. That metal-roofed log cabin building with the pillared archway over the entrance."

"It looks quite new. And the glass-paneled doors look very welcoming."

"Let's go in and check it out."

Inside they saw a large dining room surrounded by knotty pine walls covered with pictures. A long shiny wood bar with a row of stools extended along one wall. Behind the bar was a large mirror and a number of glass shelves seemingly carrying every kind of liquor made. Fresh flowers were on all of the dining tables. And hanging on one wall, looking at the crowd, was a stuffed elk head with huge antlers.

After being encouraged to sit where they'd like, they chose a table in a corner near a window. When the server arrived, they both ordered a Sam Adams dark beer and began looking over the menu. Noticing the good-looking pepperoni pizza on a nearby table, they decided to share one along with a salad.

The place was buzzing. Most people appeared to be tourists, judging from their dress, and also their speech. They seemed to be having a great time away from their everyday life.

The beers and salad soon arrived and shortly after that the bubbling pizza.

"Very good pizza," Melanie said.

"Yes, I've had it here before. But it wasn't as good as having it with you."

They ate their pizza slowly while looking at each other and smiling. And their beers went very well with the pizza.

When they left the restaurant, they could see the inspiring view of Mount Kineo in the distance and wished they could drive closer, but not today.

It was almost 2 p.m. when they left, Melanie enjoying the different perspective travelling in the opposite direction. Finally they were on David's long driveway and soon pulled up in front of the cabin.

"We've been pretty busy since we got here. What do you say we sit outside and read for a while?"

"The only problem with that is that I can't sit very close to you in those chairs. Sitting on the sofa in front of the fireplace sounds better."

"I guess you're right since this is our last afternoon here. It's pretty warm so I think I'll put on my shorts."

"I like that idea. I'll do the same."

They were soon snuggled next to each other on the sofa with the overhead ceiling light shining on their books. It wasn't too long before David reached over and kissed Melanie passionately and began to fondle her breasts. She tousled his hair and gave him a big kiss. Then her shirt was off and his lips were on her nipples. She unbuttoned his shirt and began playing with the hair on his chest., twisting and curling it.

"Why do men have hair on their chests and women don't?"

"I guess we've got to have something that turns you on."

"You mean besides your attractive face, your unassuming personality, and what's between your legs."

"I guess so"

"Well that certainly works for me."

One thing led to another and soon they were no longer sitting.

"I was afraid this might happen," Melanie said. "Or should I say I was hoping this might happen."

"Me too."

After about a half hour of kissing, petting, and love-making they sat up and returned to reading. It became a very peaceful afternoon.

About 4:30 David turned to Melanie. "Time to think about dinner. I told you that because I'm just a carpenter and since the name of my business is The House of David, I'm going to call this dinner The Last Supper. I'm not that religious, but I'm very spiritual, so I think that works. The only problem with the name is the word last."

"The name is very clever, but I hope it doesn't mean it's the last time we can do this."

"No, I just meant the last supper this weekend."

"That's a relief."

"But I can't think right now of when it might be possible to do this again. My family usually comes up here with me later in the summer. And winter wouldn't be a good time.

"I don't want to think about that right now."

"Me neither."

David got up from the couch and went to the kitchen, excited about preparing the 'last supper'.

CHAPTER 39

David was hoping this would be one of the best meals he'd ever made. Choosing the menu was determined by whom he was making it for. He'd purchased two filet mignons, planning to grill them. And he wanted to have his favorite scalloped potatoes, along with fresh green beans, chopped shallots, balsamic vinegar, and butter. For dessert it would be their freshly-picked raspberries smothered with the French raspberry liquor, Chambord, that he'd purchased with money he'd been saving.

He made appetizers of cherry tomatoes, cheddar cheese, salami and olives on small spears. Then he opened a bottle of white wine, pouring a glass for each of them. Placing it all on a tray, he carried it out to the patio where Melanie was enjoying the view.

"Why thank you sir. I have a tip for you but it will have to come later."

"I can hardly wait."

Returning to the kitchen, David sliced the potatoes, added the milk, cheese and spices and put them in the oven. He lit the charcoal and while the coals were getting hot, he cooked the beans in boiling water and let them drain. Then he had a few minutes to sit with Melanie and enjoy a few appetizers.

"I had to include some time to be able to sit out here. It's too nice not to have this time with you before dinner." He poured them another glass of wine.

"I've been thinking about the entire weekend and can't actually believe it has happened. No matter what happens with us, I'll cherish this time forever.," she said. "You know how Christians say they've been born again. I think I've been born again this weekend."

"That's a good description of the way I feel."

Soon the briquets were ready and he poured them on the grill, spreading them out evenly. He'd packaged some mesquite smoking chips in foil and, after brushing the grill, dropped the packet onto the hot briquets.

He checked the potatoes and found them almost done so it was time to put on the steaks. When they were done he carried them inside covered with foil.

It was time to call Melanie to the picnic table where he'd put the plates, along with a vase of lupin he'd picked along the highway.

"This looks absolutely delightful. I don't really know what else to say, except thank you very much."

"I don't know much about wine but the wine store owner recommended this Heitz Cabernet Sauvignon to go with the steaks. After taking a sip, I understand why.

"You did very well. This wine is fantastic." She held up her juice glass for a toast and they clicked across the table.

"Everything tastes so good. I'm having trouble deciding what to eat next. My steak is medium rare and perfect. And the potatoes and beans are wonderful."

"I guess I lucked out to have everything finished at the same time."

"In my experience, that takes good advanced planning."

They had another glass of wine while finishing their dinner, enjoying the birds tweeting and the trees whispering in the wind. The view of the lake included the raft David had built, and memories of the day before came flooding back.

"Let's take our usual walk around the property before we have dessert. It's so peaceful this time of the evening."

They began by heading towards the lake where a quarter moon was visible above the tree line. David squeezed Melanie's hand and drew her to him followed by a lengthy kiss, after which they turned and continued their walk.

The undergrowth was soft and crunchy underfoot and they were surrounded by beautiful green trees. "It's like being in a dream," Melanie said.

After they came full circle back to the cabin, David grabbed Melanie's hand and led her to the picnic table.

"It's time for dessert. How about some fresh raspberries?"

"I hope it will be the ones we picked today on that memorable outing?"

"That's exactly the ones I mean. And they will be marinated in a special ingredient."

"Would I know what that is?"

"It's called Chambord, something a man at our liquor store at home had once recommended to me. It's a special French liquor made with raspberries, and it has a little zing to it."

"After that wonderful walk, I probably could use a little zing."

"Good. I'll be right out with it."

Soon he came out of the cabin carrying a wooden tray with two bowls as well as a fancy, ball-shaped bottle that contained a red liquid.

"This is your special dessert that is payback for picking the raspberries as well as other activities."

"Oh. You mean we have to pay back when we do something for each other."

"Not necessarily, but it's fun."

He set the bowls in front of them along with the bottle and two small glasses.

"The glasses are there if you desire to have more of the Chambord."

She picked up her spoon and tasted the dessert. "This is fantastic. The raspberry flavors are so intense."

"That's what the Chambord does for them. And try a little in your glass. I think you'll like it straight from the bottle."

After pouring it, she commented, "It's very nice. I could get addicted."

"I already am but I don't have it very often. It's expensive, so I only have it when I'm here where the good raspberries reside."

They finished the dessert and carried their dishes to the kitchen.

"What's next on the agenda?"

"Why don't I light fire and we can sit on the rug and enjoy its crackling flames."

"That sounds delightful."

Soon they were sitting on the old orange shag rug, leaning against the large fluffy pillows propped up against the coffee table. The fire contributed to a faint orange glow around the room. Staring at it was mesmerizing.

It wasn't long before they were wrapped together enjoying lengthy kisses. Their shirts were soon off and then the rest of their clothes. They lay there for a while, just touching each other in sensitive spots. Soon it was more than that.

After their love making they lay there with only their shirts on, Melanie's partially buttoned. "I'd feel more comfortable if we could throw that thin brown blanket over us, at least up to our waists."

"No sooner said than done," David said as he covered them.

"Can we talk about what's happening with us and where we're headed?" Melanie said.

"I'm all for it."

"As you've mentioned before, we're probably not going to be able to do this again at your cabin, at least this year. And going to a motel doesn't sound right to me. It sounds more like cheating on our spouses than this does. And I think it would make us feel cheap."

"I agree. So where does that leave us? Going to lunch once in a while and meeting at Starbucks. Is that enough, after what we've just experienced?"

"Not for me. I guess we have to go along the best we can, figuring what can come next."

"We've avoided the subject of leaving our spouses. That wouldn't be too much of a problem for me if I didn't have kids. But I couldn't break up our family at this point. Maybe after they're gone."

"I couldn't either. I love our kids too much. And I guess I still love Paul in some ways but there doesn't seem to be any romantic feelings about him anymore."

"I guess we could try occasional lunches and see how it goes, and take things from there. And meet at Starbucks."

"Those sound like our only choice."

They fell asleep in each other's arms.

CHAPTER 40

A few interruptions of sleep occurred during the night but nothing like the previous night. It was more wanting to savor every moment. A lot of caressing, gentle kisses not necessarily on the other's lips, falling asleep with their hands touching the other's body.

They awoke in the morning with mixed feelings, that of having slept together but also knowing it could be the last time. Melanie's hair was hanging in her eyes and David's was tousled, pointing in all directions. They looked at each other and laughed.

Melanie put on a short cotton nightshirt and David wore his pajama bottoms, both wanting to dress relatively modestly since they didn't want to get aroused during breakfast, their last morning together.

After making coffee, David put some bacon on the cast iron skillet and the Bisquick, egg, and milk in a bowl for the pancake batter. Fresh raspberries mashed and marinated in Chambord made a great topping.

Soon a pile of pancakes and two strips of bacon were place on a plate in front of Melanie.

"This looks wonderful. What do I do with this red mixture in the bowl?"

"Put it on your pancakes. I think you'll recognize the flavor."

She smothered her pancakes with it and took a bite. "This is to die for. But I'm not ready to die yet. Maybe after I finish breakfast."

"I thought you'd like it. The raspberry topping adds to the pancakes."

"And you must have used some Chambord"

"I did."

"It's too good."

After they finished eating and were on their second cups of coffee, they stared at each other.

"What are we going to do this morning, and I'm not suggesting adult games."

"Oh, darn. I guess we'll have to go to my second choice. I'd like to recommend a ride on the raft before I disassemble it. I'd never be able to explain to Ginny why I built it for myself."

"I'd love to take a ride. That way I can admire your muscular body while you paddle me around like a queen."

"So let's get dressed for a raft ride. I think it's warm enough I'll wear my trunks."

"And I'll put on my shorts, and a top of course."

"Do you have to?"

"I do. What kind of a girl do you think I am?"

"I already know what kind of a girl you are and I like very much what I've discovered."

"I guess we'd better get this show on the road," Melanie said, as she headed for her bedroom.

They were pushing the raft into the water, Melanie climbing on, and David walking it out farther. He finally jumped on and began poling them out about a hundred yards, while Melanie enjoyed the view.

They'd brought a third cup of coffee with them, which they consumed while drifting around.

Soon it was time to head in since David still had to disassemble the raft.

They pulled it further ashore than before so it would be easier to undo the ropes. Melanie unwound them while David hauled the logs back to the pile.

When they were finished, they looked at each other and saw that they were a mess, with dirt on their hands, arms, faces and legs. They broke into laughter.

"Another shower?" Melanie asked.

"Definitely! I hope it can be as thorough as the last one."

"Let's give it a try."

Hurrying into the bathroom, David turned the water on and adjusted the temperature. After they stripped down, Melanie held onto David while stepping over the edge of the tub.

They scrubbed each other thoroughly. Then they took turns scrubbing each other's hair. After some stroking rather than scrubbing, it wasn't long before David took control of the situation and they became intertwined.

When the hot water began to turn cold, they reluctantly separated and got out.

The large towels were used to dry each other, especially in certain places.

Melanie slipped into her panties before blowing her hair dry, choosing to show off her attractive breasts. While doing this she noticed some activity on David's body, which she tried to ignore.

She was unsuccessful and they were soon entwined on the bed, relishing the intense feelings.

Their last lunch at the cabin consisted of steak sandwiches made from leftover dinner filets. Beers went well with the sandwiches as well as potatoes chips and apples.

"Finishing up his sandwich and taking a last swig of beer, David said, "I guess it's time to pack."

"Do we have to?"

"Unless you want to stay here forever."

"I do."

"Me too."

They retreated to the bedrooms to get their things together, Melanie with her small blue suitcase that ostensibly went to New York for the weekend, and David with his black duffel bag.

She placed her suitcase by the door, and when David came out of his bedroom, he had his bag slung over his shoulder. Picking up the suitcase, he headed for the car, leaving her standing there with a sad look on her face.

When he returned, she was sitting on the couch staring at the fireplace. Her legs were folded under her, revealing her attractive thighs. David immediately sat next to her and reached to caress the softness near her hips. His fingers were soon making further inroads, causing Melanie to moan in ecstasy. This was a turning point and they were soon stretched out on the couch, having one last engagement before the drive home.

"What a great sendoff for me. Do you do that with all the women you bring here?"

"No, only the ones who pass the test."

"Oh, what's the test?"

"To be beautiful, brilliant, attractive, modest and someone I'm attracted to. And you're the only one who's passed the test."

"Whew. That's a relief."

"As much as I hate to say it, as soon as you slip your shorts back on, we'd better get going."

"I guess we've delayed it as long as possible."

After locking up, they were in the car, heading south.

CHAPTER 41

It was a rather quiet drive down the west side of the lake. They occasionally grasped hands and took random glances at each other while enjoying looking at the beautiful green trees and meadows. One stretch gave them a final view of the lake as well as the blue lupin growing along the roadside.

Both were trying to absorb what had happened and wondering where their relationship could possibly could be going. When they got to the Shop'n Save, David spoke up. "I'm hungry for an ice cream sandwich."

"Me too. I'd prefer a simple one with just a graham cracker crust, not the ones covered with chocolate. Let me buy them. You've contributed a lot more than I have for the weekend. It's not a lot of money but it will make me feel better."

"All right. If you insist."

They returned to the car carrying the sandwiches wrapped in paper napkins. Sitting in the car with the doors open, they relished the cool ice cream.

After putting the napkins in the trash, they were off again.

"Next stop, Starbucks in Augusta? Are you up for it?" David said.

"For sure. It will be our last time together until we see each other again."

"Isn't that an oxymoron?"

"If it is, it's still the way I feel."

"Women have the right to keep a man guessing."

"That's true."

After a couple of hours they pulled into the Starbucks at exit 109. It was now familiar territory.

They both ordered Grande low fat mochas, Melanie paying for them, and then moving to the pickup line. They moved to the counter with the window directly in front of them.

"I hope we can continue to meet at Starbucks on Fridays, although we have to be careful to not sit next to each other if Joanne is there. We'll have to figure something out. Maybe sometimes we could be sitting on opposite sides of the store and talk to each other on our cell phones, or text each other."

"That's a great idea. Why didn't I think of that?"

"I'm just a carpenter, but occasionally I have a good idea."

"As I told you before, I definitely like your tools."

"I guess it's time to get back to the car," David said as he finished his mocha and reached for her hand as he looked directly into her eyes. "It's another hour before we have to separate. It's going to be tough."

"Yes. And we'll have to tone down our manner so it doesn't appear that we've had the most exciting adventure of our lives. At least that's what it's been for me."

"Me too."

They walked to the car, hand in hand. A short time later they stopped at a rest area so Melanie could change into her business clothes. She came out looking very dressed up.

"This feels pretty stuffy after what I've gotten used to wearing these last couple of days," she said as she climbed into the back seat of the car that had now become an Uber."

"Especially when you were running around naked."

"David, watch your language. You know we were only without clothes a few short but wonderful times."

"I know, but I couldn't resist making the comment. Some of my best memories of you are of those times, but all of the memories are great."

"Changing the subject, I hope we're going to be able to have lunch Wednesday or Thursday? Have you thought about it?"

"I have. And the bad news is that I don't think I'll be able to get away. Since I'm away today, and was also away on Friday, I'm sure my boss has work backed up for me. And because there's no way I can easily communicate with you before then, I'll have to say that we can't do it this week. But let's plan to be at Starbucks on Friday and at that point we can make arrangements for lunch next week. Believe me, it's just as hard on me as it is on you, but I can't risk doing it."

Around 4 p.m., they pulled up to Melanie's house. David jumped out and hustled around to open her door. "One last glimpse of those gorgeous legs."

"It's good you whispered. Remember we're now on sensitive turf."

"I know, but could I carry your suitcase to the front door?"

"I'd appreciate that very much. And I should have dropped an earring so I could see you tomorrow morning. That was a momentous occasion when you delivered it."

"It was for me too, David said as he smiled and winked at her.

She got her key out and unlocked the door. Pushing it open, she turned to David and said, "Here's a tip in case a neighbor is watching."

"Thank you," he said with a choked-up voice. He then walked rather briskly back to the car, struggling to hold back tears.

Melanie watched him drive off, pretending to search for the handle on the suitcase, and then moved inside. She settled onto a dining room chair trying to deal with her emotions. Zelda peeked in from the kitchen and said, "Welcome home Miss Melanie. It's so good to have you back. How was your trip."

"My presentation went very well, but it's good to be home," she lied.

"I made some lasagna for dinner, not knowing what time you'd get back."

"That sounds great, Zelda. Thank you so much. It's been a busy weekend so I'm a bit bushed."

"I can imagine. All of those meetings. They can wear you out."

If she only knew the kind of meetings she'd had.

"The kids should be home soon. Maybe you could put out a snack for them before you leave. I'm going upstairs to unpack and take a nap."

"You go ahead. I'll take care of the kids."

Melanie went slowly upstairs, dragging her suitcase behind her. She wanted to get her Moosehead Lake clothes hidden quickly. After doing that and changing into jeans and a t-shirt, she plopped on the bed and closed her eyes.

A half hour later Josh was shaking her arm saying, "Wake up Mom. I have lots to tell you."

"Oh, hi Sweetie." She pulled herself up while yawning, and kissed him on his cheek. "Yes, I definitely want to hear all about your weekend." Something to distract me, she thought.

Slowly moving down the stairs, she entered the family room. Nellie was sitting on the sofa, texting. Melanie slid next to her and gave her a kiss on the cheek. Nellie turned, said hi, and went back to texting.

Josh spoke up. "Mom, I got a triple on Saturday. And I caught a fly ball when I was playing left field. Dad was so pleased, he took me to the ice cream store where I got my favorite; a double cone of mint chocolate chip."

"That's wonderful. Sounds like you might be one of the team's star players."

"I wouldn't say that, but at least I'm pretty good."

That caught Melanie off guard. Had she been doing something good or something bad? Good for her immediate gratification, but maybe bad for her marriage. She pushed that out of her mind, thinking she'd deal with it later. For now, she was too worn out, both physically and emotionally, to think about it.

By then it was 5:30. Time to work on dinner. She moved to the kitchen and took the lasagna out of the fridge. It wouldn't take long to heat it up after Paul came home. It looked very tasty with the cheese sprinkled on top. And the bread needed slicing and spread with butter and chopped garlic.

She mixed a few tomatoes, some slices of cucumber and shreds of lettuce with an Italian dressing in a wooden bowl and put it into the fridge.

"Now I get to sit down and have a glass of Chardonnay while waiting for Paul," she muttered to herself.

She moved to the family room and crashed on the comfy sofa.

CHAPTER 42

Paul came bounding through the door wearing a broad smile, heading directly for Melanie. He pulled her to him, put his arm around her waist, and gave her a kiss on the lips.

"Wow, what have you been drinking?" she said.

"Absolutely nothing. I wanted to show you that I missed you."

"I missed you too. It's good to be home," she lied.

"Could we sit in the family room and watch the news together? I'll mix you a gin and tonic."

"That sounds good. I've got dinner almost ready so it will be easy to put on the table."

Soon they were sitting on the leather sofa, their drinks within easy reach on the coffee table. Paul turned on the six-o'clock news and they sat there enjoying their cocktails with Paul occasionally leaning over and kissing her on the cheek.

What's got into him, she wondered? Could he have taken a testosterone pill? This is not the usual Paul.

When the news ended, Melanie got up and picked up her glass. "It will be a few minutes before dinner is ready, and since you just refreshed your drink that should keep you busy."

"Come here," he said. "One more kiss." She leaned down and gave him a peck on the lips. Then turned and moved towards the kitchen.

Where was he going with this? It must be one of those rare nights when he wants to make love, she thought. She'd already experienced sex twice that day but decided she had no choice.

After heating up the lasagna and garlic bread, she announced dinner was ready. She'd placed a few roses in a low vase on the table, along with four plates.

"I'm going to dish up the lasagna and pass around the garlic bread and salad. You kids have to have a reasonable amount of salad. I'll be checking."

When everyone's plates were dished up, Paul finally said, "How was your trip? You seem to be rather quiet about it. Was the meeting good? And was your talk successful?

"Sorry I haven't mentioned it. I'm just kind of worn out. It was a great meeting and my presentation went very well."

She thought about her presentation. "It was a very busy time and I'm not used to the pace," she said and meant it.

"Well, I hope it was worthwhile and you didn't overdo it."

"No, I'll be fine. Just sitting down with you and having that drink helped me relax."

"I enjoyed it too. We don't do that often enough."

How can we when you're so engrossed in your games, she thought.

"By the way, there are no games on tonight, so I was hoping we could sit down together and watch a movie."

"I'd love that. You find one you'd like and I'll hope to stay awake."

"I'll check into it while you do the dishes."

Has he ever volunteered to help with the dishes?

When the dishes were finished Melanie went into the family room and sat next to Paul. He put his arm around her and kissed her on the cheek.

"I think I found a good one. It's *Mission Impossible*, a thriller with Tom Cruz, the kind we like."

What he really meant was that it was the kind he liked. But she felt she owed it to him. Especially after having the greatest weekend of her life. Hopefully this would erase some of her guilt.

Paul started the movie and Melanie leaned against his shoulder.

"This is really great. Are you enjoying it, honey?"

"What? Oh yes, the action is keeping me awake." Actually she kept drifting off.

He hit the pause button. "Would you like something to sip on? Maybe some Drambuie or Kahlua? I know you like both of those."

"A great idea. I'd love some Kahlua on ice. Maybe the coffee in it will keep me awake."

The movie finally ended, along with the Kahlua.

"I can tell you're probably ready to go to bed. Shall we head upstairs?"

"That sounds like a good idea. I'll put these glasses in the kitchen and follow you."

"Okay. See you in bed." He smiled.

After doing her nighttime bathroom routine, she put on a nightgown, knowing that would make it easier for Paul. He was already in bed so she slid in next to him. He immediately rolled over and put his arm around her. They began kissing, or actually is was he who began kissing. She had to respond the best she could.

"It's so nice to be so close to you," Paul said.

"Yes, we haven't done this for a while." She didn't know whether to interject that comment, but couldn't help it.

"It hasn't been that long, has it?"

"I guess not. It just seems like it."

After caressing her breasts for a while, he rolled on top and soon found what he was searching for. After a short bit of activity, with Melanie feigning her interest, Paul finished and rolled over.

"That was wonderful," he said, and fell asleep.

Is that what she'd have to put up with for the rest of her life? Hopefully the memories of the weekend would sustain her. She turned her head away from Paul and began to relive some of the weekend activities, not just the sexual ones, until she fell asleep.

. . .

David arrived home, making sure he looked like he'd been working on the property, wearing his old jeans and a long-sleeved work shirt. He took time to unload the back of the car, not wanting to face Ginny, even though she shouldn't have any reason to suspect anything. He walked into the kitchen where she was busy preparing dinner and kissed her on the cheek.

"That's nice. I missed you," she said.

"I missed you, too," he replied. "But it was a good time to be there to de-winterize things. And I managed to catch a few trout. Not enough to bring home, but enough to fry for breakfast."

"At least you caught some. What did you catch them with?"

"Just worms. I guess they were tired of flies." He continued the lying.

"So what else kept you busy?"

"I was only up there for two days. I got there late Friday and left mid-morning today and went to work. And it rained yesterday so I was busy with the leaks. What is this? Some sort of an interrogation?"

"Not at all. I just wondered what I missed. What about raspberries? Did you get a chance to pick any?"

"No. Too busy with cleaning and repairs." He was glad he'd rinsed the raspberry juice out of his t-shirt.

"Take your bag upstairs and unpack. Then come down and have a beer. Dinner will be ready soon. I made spaghetti and meat balls, one of your favorites, with garlic bread."

"Sounds great." He got up and grabbed a beer out of the fridge. He couldn't help wonder what Melanie was doing. Was she having as much trouble coming down from the clouds as he was?"

CHAPTER 43

She awoke on Tuesday morning, burying her head in her pillow and realizing there was no cabin, no beautiful lake, and especially, no David. How could she survive? It was already 10:30. She never slept this long! It was supposed to be a normal workday so she'd have to get moving.

As she climbed into the shower she was aware that it was less then 24 hours ago that she was still at the cabin, enjoying a very refreshing shower with David. Actually much more than refreshing!

She brushed her hair into a ponytail, put on normal workday clothes and headed down stairs.

When she arrived in the kitchen, she could see that Paul had set out breakfast for the kids and he must have left them lunch money. Everything seemed to be in order. Life as usual. The kids obviously got out of the house with their backpacks.

It was too quiet. No David to have coffee with. No fancy breakfast or even a nice Danish. It was depressing. How could she wait until Friday to see him? She had to settle for a bowl of Cheerios topped with a sliced banana, drowned in milk, and a glass of orange juice.

After finishing breakfast, she cleaned up the dishes and headed upstairs to collect her purse and check her hair.

It wasn't long before she was on Congress Street turning into the alley. Too late to get a parking space. She had to drive a block away and park on the street. Upon entering her building, she decided to hike up the stairs. Maybe that would stimulate some energy, which she badly needed.

Although it was a shortened day, it seemed much longer than usual. Too much daydreaming and not much work done. Hopefully things would get better as the week went on.

∎ ∎ ∎

By Friday Melanie hadn't accomplished much at work but found time for a lot of thinking. All she knew was that she wanted to be with David as much as possible, which was looking like not very much.

But at least it was Friday, and hopefully he'd be at Starbucks. She kept watching the clock. It was 9 a.m. She'd leave at 9:45, so she found some busy work to keep herself occupied until then.

Soon she was out the door and running down the stairs.

∎ ∎ ∎

David woke up Friday morning, realizing what was up for the day. During the week he'd managed to keep busy with the jobs that had backed up. But he made sure he could be at Starbucks by 10 a.m.

As he dressed he thought about how torturous the week had been, not being able to get Melanie out of his mind. Ginny was her usual self, keeping things going around the house and preparing meals. A couple of times she approached him and gave him a peck on the cheek, but that was all. Nothing amorous. And he couldn't bring himself to lure her into the bedroom.

Soon he was out the door and off to the job, hoping the first few hours would go fast. He was installing windows and each one was a separate job, so he could adjust the timing to fit with Starbucks.

At 9:35, he was in his car and off to Congress Street. He luckily found a parking space around the corner from the coffee house and made a beeline for the door. He wanted to be there first so he could watch her walk by.

He was sitting at the window counter, not the usual inside counter, sipping his mocha and there she was, moving quickly towards the entrance, with a slight smile on her face. She turned and when she saw him she broke into a broad smile, but extinguished it quickly.

David decided to remain at the window, taking a chance. He could see that only a few of the nearby counter stools were occupied so she wouldn't have a problem finding a seat. Although he was very tempted, he knew he shouldn't turn to look at her.

She was sitting three seats away, reaching for her phone.

David's phone vibrated. It had to be her.

"Hi." He took the risk to answer that way.

"Hi. I missed you."

"Same for me. Terribly, as a matter of fact."

"Me too. I don't dare look at you, although I'd love to."

"Same here. But it's great to hear your voice."

"I had a difficult time trying to follow up on my accounts. Ideas weren't coming forth like they usually do."

"Well at least you weren't occasionally pounding your thumb with a hammer."

She laughed. "Did you have to go to the ER?"

"Not quite. But if you'd have been the nurse or doctor, I'd definitely have gone."

"And I would've had to examine you, so I'd make you take off your clothes."

"That would be great if you were the only one in the room."

"Don't get me aroused. It's bad enough thinking about the weekend."

"I'll change the subject. Are you available for lunch next week?"

"It's at the top of my list. Could we do it on Wednesday. Thursday is too long to wait."

"I'll meet you at CVS at noon."

"I'd like to change the subject. And don't get upset if you think I'm being too forward," she said, still speaking to him on her iPhone. "I've been craving at least a hug from you. I had an idea that I checked out yesterday."

"This sounds intriguing. What are you suggesting?"

"There are two unisex bathrooms down the hall. I propose that I go to one of them and you stop by fairly soon afterwards and knock three times and I'll let you in."

"Are you serious?"

"Very."

"Then I'm willing."

"I don't mean we'd do anything intimate. Just that we'd get to hug and hold each other briefly, although doing something sexy sounds pretty exciting."

"Let's do it. Life is too short not to take chances."

"What if someone wants to get in while we're there?"

"I'll figure that out if and when it happens."

"OK. I'm going now since I can see that no one is waiting. Hopefully one of the bathrooms will be empty. Watch to see which one I go in."

He could see that she entered the one on the right. He slid off his stool and walked down the hall. Then three knocks on the door.

It opened and there she was, her blue eyes shining and a wide grin on her full lips. She'd partially unbuttoned her blouse so he could see that she wasn't wearing a bra.

The bathroom was exceptionally clean so they both felt comfortable standing there.

"I'm here waiting for you."

"I can see that." He extended his arms and pulled her to him. They embraced and shared a very long kiss.

"Oh how I missed this," he said.

"No more than I have," she said.

I'm glad you're not wearing lipstick or I'd be in trouble when I leave."

She laughed.

He reached to fondle her breasts while giving her another long kiss. Maybe that was a mistake because it just aroused them further. He could feel that her nipples were very enlarged and she noticed a bulge in his pants, which she stroked.

"We have to stop. We can't go any further," he said.

"I know. But at least I got to be held by you."

She pulled away and began buttoning her blouse.

"I was surprised to find you not wearing a bra."

"I normally do, at work, but I had other things in mind today, which you helped satisfy."

"I guess we'll have to move on. I'll say goodbye with another hug and head back to work."

"I guess we have no other choice. But I can hardly wait until Wednesday."

They embraced one more time and then David moved towards the door. "Why don't you stand behind the door so if someone's outside, they won't see you. And then lock the door when I leave. If someone's there, I'll make up some excuse as to why it's still locked. You can leave shortly after that." He blew her a kiss and was gone.

A man was standing next to the door and reached to open it after David came out.

"How come this is still locked?"

"There's another person there. I was helping them put on a bandage but they'll be out soon."

"Yeah, sure. A great excuse."

Soon Melanie emerged, saw the man, and walked quickly past him, saying nothing. She was out the front door, heading for her office, and not knowing whether she felt more heavy-hearted or more upbeat. She decided she felt better having been with him.

CHAPTER 44

Melanie had to make an extra effort throughout the weekend to keep from thinking about David. She even went to church, which didn't happen often.

"Are you feeling OK," Paul asked her. "You never go to church."

"I know. I was just in the mood today."

"Speaking of moods, you've been acting kind of glum lately. Did anything bad happen at the conference last weekend?"

"No, not really. I guess it's a let-down having my presentation over with, especially after spending so much time preparing." She hated to lie but what else could she do?

. . .

Wednesday didn't come around soon enough. At 11.30 she was out the door, heading for the bus stop. No checking out the boutique, no stopping at Starbucks. A lot of people were bustling around on the sidewalks, probably heading somewhere for lunch. She made her way through the crowds and arrived at the bus stop to find a line of people. When the blue bus pulled up, she boarded and headed for the rear.

What was going on? She seemed to have lost control of her life. She had to have a David fix. A few weeks ago she was a normal person, living a normal life. And where was she now? Was this what drug addicts felt like when they needed a fix?

But she'd be with David soon.

She stepped off the bus and hurried to the pharmacy. Arriving at her lookout location, she began to browse and keep an eye on the entrance.

There he was. She wanted to rush to greet him but decided that would be unwise, so she moved slowly.

. . .

David struggled with the weekend chores. Mowing and edging the lawn, trimming the plants and flowers, anything to get his mind off of her. The family went on an outing at a nearby lake on Sunday. While sitting at a picnic table eating his sandwich, he couldn't help but remember a similar table at the cabin with Melanie sitting across from him. Everything he did reminded him of her. And the ploy she came up with at Starbucks was very imaginative. He loved it, even though it was a little unsettling when the guy at the door questioned him. He thought he handled it well.

. . .

On Wednesday, it was time to head to CVS. At 9:30 he left the job site and drove there. By now it felt like a routine shopping place to him. Walking through the door, he looked for that lovely face with the deep blue eyes and the blond pony tail.

. . .

Melanie saw him enter so she moved to the front of the store. He reached his hand out and touched her briefly. Then they moved towards the checkout counter, Melanie picked up a small package of mixed nuts and David, a candy bar. Soon they were out the door, David moving somewhat ahead as they walked towards his car. She pretended to be getting into the next car and then quickly opened his door and slid in.

He leaned over and gave her a quick kiss. "Let's get this show on the road," he exclaimed.

"I'm ready. Actually, I'm ready for anything with you."

"Anything?"

"Yes." She touched his arm.

It wasn't long before they approached the restaurant. David pulled behind the building and parked. After getting out, he quickly moved to her side to let her out. Soon they were heading for the front door arm in arm.

"I hope we can get as quiet a table as we did last time."

"Any table works if you're sitting across from me," said David.

They found an ideal location with a water view. The table was set for two with a linen tablecloth and fresh flowers. The server came and they ordered the house Chardonnay, as before.

The wine was soon placed in front of them, as were the menus.

"Give me a wave when you're ready to order."

"Thanks, we'll do that," David said.

They decided to share the regular size lobster salad. They weren't in the mood for a lot of food. David just wanted to sit there and stare at her. She did the same with him.

The server brought the salad to the table, along with two smaller plates to divide it up.

"This looks delicious. Is it going to be enough for you? A big growing boy and a carpenter as well."

"I think it will do. Now I'm only hungry for you."

"That's a nice thing to say. Is it alright to toast to that?" She picked up her wine glass and held it towards him.

He clicked and they both took sips.

"I keep thinking about all those wonderful adventures. The raft, the drive to Rockwood, the raspberry picking, and of course all the other stuff," Melanie said.

"You mean there was other stuff?"

"You know very well what I mean. So where do we go from here?" Melanie said.

"I have something for you." He reached into his pocket and

pulled out a small tissue-paper-wrapped package and handed it to her. "Go ahead. Open it."

She pulled away the taped portion and unfolded the tissue. Reaching inside, she gasped. "Oh, it's beautiful!" It was a polished peach-colored flat stone with a silver chain attached.

"I found the stone in the water sometime last year and was wondering what to do with it. That is until you came along. It's made of quartzite and I polished it in my rock polisher."

"It's so smooth, and the color is beautiful. Thank you. I'll treasure it always." She leaned across the table and gave him a big kiss.

"So getting back to our agenda. What's up?"

"I was going to ask you the same thing. "

"I guess it's Starbucks day after tomorrow. And lunch here next Wednesday?"

"Doesn't sound very exciting, but at least we get to see each other."

"I'm sure a creative idea will come that will allow us to have more time together."

"I hope so. Otherwise we might wither up and die for lack of love."

"Don't say that. We'll think of something."

Soon they were approaching his car. When they got to her door, he put his arm around her waist and pulled her to him, giving her a very passionate kiss.

Responding, she said, "Wow! What a pleasant surprise."

"Just something I've been longing to do."

Soon they were in the car, holding hands on occasion while heading for CVS.

"I'm glad you're good at driving with one hand. And remember, I've got both hands to work with. She reached over and teased him.

He let her off at CVS and drove back to his job site while Melanie took the next bus back to her office.

CHAPTER 45

They had their Friday rendezvous at Starbucks, using cell phones to communicate but skipping the bathroom interlude. Too risky to repeat. When they departed, they reminded each other of the Wednesday lunch date.

David spent the weekend in his shop. He had several orders that kept him busy. On Wednesday he dressed in what had become his Wednesday lunch outfit of nice jeans and a buttoned short sleeve shirt. He had to be careful to not dress too fancy since he'd be working in those clothes.

"Got a hot date today?" his boss asked.

"No. Just lunch with a friend. I don't want to be too unkempt when I meet him." To be safe, David used the male gender for the lunch meeting.

"Well don't drink too much. You don't want to cut your finger off when you get back."

"I'll be extra careful. Probably only have one beer."

• • •

When he arrived at CVS, he sauntered over to the entrance, anticipating that beautiful smile on her face. Heading down the cosmetic aisle, he saw her approach him. He grasped her hand and they moved towards the door.

"I've been looking forward to this all week. You make my life so full."

"The same for me," she said.

David noticed that she was a little quieter than usual but maybe she was having a bad day at work.

They pulled up behind the restaurant and after getting out of the car, they embraced and shared a lengthy kiss.

They were searching for a quiet secluded table. The corner one overlooking the ocean was perfect.

They sat down and Melanie signaled for the server. "We both want a glass of your house Chardonnay please."

She usually wasn't that forward. She generally asked him what he'd like.

She was looking around the room rather than at him. What's up he wondered?

"You're not your usual self. Is something wrong?

Tears began flowing down her cheeks.

"I have some bad news. I've known for the last couple of days and couldn't think how to tell you."

"What is it?"

"Paul's been transferred to his company's head office in Columbus, Ohio and he needs to be there quickly. They have an urgent problem that he's particularly good at dealing with. We'll be flying there tomorrow to find some temporary housing. I don't know how long it will be until I get back, but I won't have my office here anymore. The lease will be up next week and it makes no sense to renew it, other than to meet you at Starbucks. And I can't do business here at our home, leaving the kids to fend for themselves in Ohio. We have to get them in their new schools as soon as possible."

"Wow! Did I hear you correctly? What are we going to do?"

"It will be difficult to make these Wednesday dates when I'm in Ohio. We'll just have to see if we can work something out. At this time, I haven't been able to come up with anything creative. I've had a couple of good cries at my office the last two days so I'm a step ahead of you in the grief department."

"It must have been quite a shock."

"It certainly was. But here I am thinking only about myself and how this will affect my life when I should also be thinking of you."

"I noticed something was wrong when I first saw you in CVS but just brushed it off."

"I've had a chance to think about it a lot. For a way to meet, I could say I'm going to New York and instead come up here but where would I stay, and what could we do?"

"I can see that not living here will make it difficult."

"And there's no way I can get in touch with you. We have no communication channel except Starbucks."

"We had our discussion about dissolving our marriages and we decided against that."

"So we have to make our marriages work, mainly for our children's sake," she said.

"Does this mean we won't be able to see each other again?"

"Certainly in the near term. I don't see any way around it."

He thought for a few minutes. "I guess not."

"We could meet at Moosehead Lake next summer."

"That's too far ahead to even think about," he said.

"I'm not very hungry but I think we should try to eat something."

"I guess so. I'll try the fish and chips. I don't feel like having anything fancy."

"That sounds good to me too."

They placed their orders and soon the fish baskets were in front of them."

"It's pretty good fish but I'll probably never have fish and chips again."

"Me neither."

David noticed that Melanie was occasionally fondling the necklace he'd given her.

When they finished their meals they decided to share a dessert. Something they could do together. They chose a hot fudge sundae with nuts sprinkled on top.

When it arrived, they decided to feed each other across the table, first checking to make sure no one would notice. But even if someone did, they didn't care.

"Who gets the first bite."

"Definitely you do because you're so attractive." He took a scoop and passed it over to her waiting mouth. She engulfed it and they chuckled, the first time that day.

"This definitely will be my favorite dessert from now on. It will keep you with me always," she said.

"I'll remember that. We might be eating them at the same time but many miles apart. A special connection."

Melanie slid an extra-large scoop in his mouth, catching him off guard.

"That's for surprising me in the shower, lifting me up the way you did. But it was a very pleasant surprise."

"I could never forget."

"And this one is for pinning me down on the logging trail in the rain and taking advantage of me." The large scoop smeared around the outside of his mouth.

"If we're getting even, what about the time you climbed onto me. I'm not used to having a woman do that." He pressed a large scoop into her mouth and they both broke out laughing.

When they finished the sundae, they grabbed each other's hands and held them for a few moments.

"I can't believe this is happening. Couldn't you have taken another flight that day so we wouldn't have met? I wonder if our experience is anything like climbing a mountain? Moving upward, you finally reach the top and then you have to begin the descent. I think today is the descent for us. But what you want to remember is the climb. And I know I had a great climb last weekend. Maybe we even reached the summit a few times."

"We definitely did! I know I'll never be able to climb another mountain, except with you. That isn't looking very likely at this point. But we can hope."

They paid the bill and walked out hand in hand. When they got to the car, David spun her around, pressing her back against the closed car door and leaning against her, his mouth on hers.

When they pulled apart, he said, "I wish we could do it in the back seat."

"In the parking lot?"

"Just kidding. My desires and what is realistic are two different things."

"I like your desires but we know it wouldn't work. Too much of a risk."

"I know." He opened her door and as she moved in he leaned over and planted another kiss while his hand was massaging her breasts.

"Just something to remember."

"If you get to, so do I," she said as her right hand reached below his belt.

"We'd better get going or something's bound to happen."

"Is this my last Uber ride with you as my driver."

"It could be, but I hope not."

"But this time I get to sit in the front seat with you. No more screeching to a quick stop though. I thought we were dead. But you saved me."

"I guess I did more than that to you."

At the bus stop they waved goodbye. A very painful scene for both of them. He pulled away with tears in his eyes as she gave him another wave. She boarded the bus and went to the rear, taking a seat at the window as her tears began to flow.

CHAPTER 46

SIX YEARS LATER

Paul was sitting on the sofa reading the Sunday *New York Times Magazine* when he called out to Melanie. "Honey, listen to this. Do you remember that guy who made furniture in his garage? I think you bought that nice chair from him."

He heard a crash in the kitchen. "What was that?"

"Oh, nothing. The frying pan just slipped out of my hand. Nothing broken. So what about the guy?"

"There's an article in the *New York Times Magazine* about how he developed a nice hand-crafted furniture business that grew from nothing in his garage to a thriving business. He claims he's just a carpenter but other people certainly don't think so. He has five craftsmen working for him housed in a large new building including a showroom. He's apparently done very well from what I'm reading."

She rushed into the family room and sat next to Paul. "Does the article include his picture?"

"Yes, there are several photos and one of them is just him. See if you recognize him."

She leaned over his shoulder and stared at the photo.

"That's him."

He looked so handsome and still trim. His blond hair partially combed to the side and that appealing smile.

"I'd like to read the article when you're through."

"You actually went to his garage to get the chair."

"Yes. I guess that was the beginning of a thriving business."

"He says that something happened to him about six years ago that inspired him and gave him the confidence to pursue this more as a business instead of a hobby. He wouldn't say what that was but he says it's like climbing a mountain and he's heading for the summit. He was going nowhere until this event happened but he's been climbing upward ever since. He said he may never get to the summit, in fact he doesn't seem to want to get there. It's too much of a letdown afterwards, he says. But he seems to be enjoying the climb.

She had to control her emotions while Paul was reading to her. She couldn't hold back a few tears, so she turned her head away and told Paul to be sure to save the article for her.

She went upstairs to the bathroom, locked the door, sat on the toilet seat and began sobbing. She couldn't figure out whether they were sad sobs or happy ones. Probably a little of both she decided.

She knew all along what a talented person he was but she never imagined he'd be so successful and able to quit being both a carpenter and an Uber driver. His family must be very proud of him, she thought. She fondled the stone hanging around her neck. She wore it every day.

Paul asked her once where she got it and why she wore it so much. She said she saw it at a boutique store on Congress Street and fell in love with it. She told him some people wore crosses and she wore a stone.

When Paul passed the article to her, she sat down and read through it slowly. He apparently became nationally known when a person from New York saw one of his pieces in someone's home and tracked him down. The person gave him an order for quite a few pieces. That gave him the incentive to develop some time-saving techniques, allowing him to make enough money to quit his other jobs. How wonderful, she thought.

The article said that getting more of his pieces out in the world led to more business and soon he couldn't handle it in his garage. He rented a larger space for a while and more recently built his own building, a combination of a shop and a showroom. He'd won several awards at furniture shows in New York.

So he's now going to New York, she thought. Too bad they never connected there. Or maybe it was good they didn't. Who knows where their relationship might have gone?

. . .

About a week later, Melanie was sitting at the breakfast table with a cup of coffee. Paul was at work, Nellie was off to college at Bowdoin in Brunswick, Maine, and Josh was a senior in high school. Her family was disappearing. Having her children around was a big help in getting over her encounter with David. But Josh would probably be going to college next year, although he wasn't the student that Nellie was. He might stay in Columbus and attend the community college. She'd deal with the idea of him leaving if and when it happened.

An idea entered her head: She'd been thinking of going to Brunswick to visit Nellie to see how things were going. Nellie was doing fine and they texted now and then, but Melanie thought seeing her situation first hand would make her feel better. She'd fly into Portland, rent a car, and head north from there.

She suddenly realized she could stop at The House of David! It would be good to see David again. She missed him every day but she knew she wouldn't be going there to rekindle their relationship. That was over. But seeing him climbing his mountain would be great.

After checking with Nellie, she booked a flight from Columbus to Portland for the next weekend. She sounded anxious for her mom's visit. Melanie would spend two nights in Brunswick and then drive back to Portland. The drive back from Brunswick to the airport was just a little over an hour so she'd have plenty of time to stop at The House of David.

CHAPTER 47

She arrived at the Portland Skyway airport at 10 a.m. on Friday and was bussed to the Avis facility. With little hassle, she was off to Brunswick, bringing back many good memories. The anticipation of driving the memorable route aroused her. She'd have to stop at the Brunswick Starbucks and have a mocha. Too bad David couldn't be sitting next to her.

She walked into the coffee shop, purchased her mocha and moved to the counter in front of the window. She tried to remember what they had talked about when they were there. Probably nothing much except she remembered she couldn't get her mind off of what was happening, going to a remote cabin with a man who wasn't her husband. But what a man he was. Good memories!

After finishing her mocha, she left with mixed feelings, partly good ones about the weekend but also a disappointment that it had to end so quickly.

She spent a delightful weekend at Bowdoin with Nellie who took her to see her dorm room and then a tour of the campus. The spired red-brick buildings were surrounded by tall spruce trees scattered among beautiful green lawns. The two of them went out to lunch and dinner every day, having a great seafood dinner at the well-known Indigo Coastal Shanty. The first night they saw a play produced by the college drama department and the second, a production at the Historic Ritz Theater.

Nellie was back in classes Monday morning while Melanie was checking out of her motel room. While she was offered a free continental breakfast, she decided to get her coffee and the wonderful coffee cake at the Brunswick Starbucks instead.

Soon she was sitting at the counter, again reminiscing about that special weekend. So many wonderful things to remember. Those thoughts had kept her going for that past six years. She knew that the relationship couldn't be re-kindled. That was too long ago. But it would be good to see David. Hopefully he'd be there instead of in New York at a furniture show. But even if he had been in the big city he should be back at work by Monday, she hoped.

She gave the address to Siri on her iPhone and was directed to his place. There it was, a beautiful white clapboard-sided building with a tree-lined asphalt parking area in front. The large House of David sign was above the doors and below that, in smaller letters, was Home of Unique Furniture Designs. The single word WELCOME was printed on the double glass doors.

She entered and saw a receptionist sitting at a desk near the front of the showroom. She rose and approached Melanie.

"Welcome to House of David. Please feel free to look around and let me know if I can help you."

"I was hoping to see your manager, Mr. Stevens."

"Oh, he's also the owner. May I tell him what this is about?"

"I purchased a chair from him a number of years ago and saw the article in the New York Times Magazine section. I thought I'd stop by and see how his business has grown."

"Let me check with him. I believe he's in his office. May I ask your name?

"It's Melanie, Melanie Johnson."

"I'll be right back," she said, before opening his office door.

Soon a tall, handsome man emerged and looked around. "Melanie? Is that really you?" He moved quickly towards her and grasped her hands as he leaned over and kissed her on the cheek.

"David. I couldn't miss this opportunity to see you. You're as good-looking as ever."

"I think you're even better looking. What brings you here?"

"You mean besides you? My daughter just started at Bowdoin this fall and I came up for a visit. I had this brilliant idea to stop by the famous 'House of David'."

"You've come to the right place."

"My husband saw the article about you in the New York Times Magazine, and I was so thrilled to read about what you've accomplished."

"It's all your fault. I hope you guessed that the reference I made to the special event six years ago was about our weekend. You completely changed my life, giving me the confidence to develop what you see here. You made me feel like more than just a carpenter."

"You changed me too," she said. "My business has been very successful due to some new ideas I presented to the marketing people in New York. And I see that you go to New York occasionally for a furniture show. Too bad you didn't do that back then."

"You're right. But I hope you got the message about climbing the mountain. I said that during the interview in hopes that you might read the article and know it was you climbing with me."

"And that's exactly what happened. It gave me the motivation to stop by."

"Can I show you around the showroom? It's a bit larger than the one I used to have when you purchased the chair."

"I'd love that."

He took hold of her arm and directed her into the large area filled with exquisite furniture displays.

"You've been very productive."

"As you might have read, I now have five master woodworkers making most of the furniture. I get to do the designs, which is the part I love."

"Did you ever think back then of how far this could go?"

"No, not until I met you. You inspired me."

"You are very kind to say that. I guess I'd better get going. I have a 3 p.m. flight."

"Let me walk you to the door."

"I'd love that."

When they got to the door, he held it open with his back while he grasped her hands, and leaned over to kiss her on the cheek. "I can't thank you enough for stopping by. You've made my day, my week, my month and also my year."

She reached inside the top of her blouse and pulled out the necklace. "I wear this every day."

"I'm so glad."

She leaned towards him again and whispered in his ear, "I'll always love you," She turned quickly and headed towards the car, hiding her tears.

ACKNOWLEDGEMENTS

I'd like to acknowledge invaluable assistance and editing from my fiction-writing coach Kit Crumb, book designer Chris Molé, my cousin Carol, my son Robert, and my wife Susan.

∾

ABOUT THE AUTHOR

BILL SILFVAST is a well-known laser scientist/professor who spent his career at Bell Laboratories and the University of Central Florida, where he was the author of over 100 technical papers and two technical books. In addition to his published first novel, *Focused to Kill, The Key,* and *Undercover,* a sequel to *The Key* will be available soon.

Soon to be released:

UNDERCOVER

Sequel to *The Key*

CHAPTER 1

At 6 a.m. on Monday, Roger Davidson walked down the dimly lit hallway to his office. He was usually the first person to arrive in the building.

After punching in the pass code, he pressed the fingerprint pad and looked into the facial recognition screen. The green light came on, his door clicked open, and he entered.

The office wasn't large. Just enough room for his gray metal desk and a few chairs. No pictures on the walls but he cherished the framed family photo on his desk. His top-secret information was stored in the secure locked file drawer.

Sitting in his chair, he reached to open the combination padlock on the drawer, needing some classified papers for a meeting. He noticed the dial of the lock was not set on the number he'd left it on the previous Friday! After locking the drawer at the end of every day, he always rotated the dial to a new number and made a note of that in his wallet. It should have been on 26 but it was on 17. Also he'd left the padlock hanging at a slight angle but today it was vertical. He couldn't be sure of the angle, but he was sure he'd left the dial on 26.

He wondered how someone could have broken in? Maybe it was possible to steal his seven-digit key-punch code. But the fingerprint and facial recognition software were supposed to be extremely secure.

He'd have to report his concern to Daniel Miller, the head of his directorate. The top-secret laser handgun project was one of the most protected secret weapons of the US military and he couldn't ignore the possibility of a break-in.

His boss also thought an intrusion was unlikely but the possibility had to be brought to the attention of the Jet Propulsion Laboratory director, Graham Wilson.

The Director immediately ordered a fingerprint test of Roger's office and found only Roger's prints. He was in an uncomfortable position. The chance that it was a theft was very slim. But if it did occur, it would most likely be a JPL employee and they couldn't let word get out or they would never be able to apprehend the person.

He got in touch with FBI Director Charles Finley on a secure line. "You say you have a possible break-in regarding some material relating to one of our most highly classified military programs," Finley said.

"That's correct sir. One of our key technologists entered his office yesterday morning and noticed that the padlock on his secure file drawer had possibly been compromised. His office is protected by a key-punch, a fingerprint screening, and a facial recognition test."

"That's a very secure system."

"We think it is and yet this problem occurred. His office was examined for fingerprints and only his were found."

"This definitely sounds like something we should investigate but we'll have to be careful that we don't let anyone at JPL know about it for fear of having the possible culprit go to ground."

"The only people who know are the person who's office is in question, the head of his directorate, and the head of JPL."

"That's good. Let's keep it that way. It could be nothing but we definitely have to look into it. I'll get my three assistant directors together and we'll determine where we should go with this."

"That sounds good Director Finley. We'll look forward to hearing from you."

"You will. That's all for now." He closed the call.

. . .

FBI Director Finley waived his three assistant directors into his office.

"Greetings Nick, Al and Darrell," he said as he shook hands with each of them. "Please come in and sit down around the table."

As they entered they enjoyed the view of the National Mall and also the Washington Monument through the large windows behind the directors desk.

"A nice day to have this view," said Nick.

"I guess it's nice out there. It seems I'm always too busy to appreciate it."

"I can imagine that."

"I'll get right to the point of the meeting," he said looking at Al and Darrell sitting on one of the love seats and Nick next to him on the other.

"First of all, I want to stress that what I'm going to say cannot go beyond the three of you in this room. Partially because we don't know whether it actually occurred but also because we can't let the culprit know that we know, if indeed it did occur. I hope that's very clear. No discussion with anyone."

"We can handle that, Chuck. Mum's the word.," Al said.

"We have an indication that a break-in might have occurred in an office of one of our senior technologists at the Jet Propulsion Lab in Pasadena. Top secret documents regarding the development of one of our highest priority weapons systems might have been accessed."

"That sounds very serious," Nick said.

"I want to stress that we don't know for certain. Hence one of the reasons for keeping it very private. What is important is that we come up with a plan of how to investigate this without alerting anyone at JPL, other than the three people who are aware of it, and they are sworn to secrecy."

"So what happens next?"

"I'm looking for creative ideas as to how we should approach this investigation. Any thoughts on the matter?"